279516

Dustin Grubbs

TAKE

Two!

Dustin Grubbs

TAKE Two!

John J. Bonk

LITTLE, BROWN AND COMPANY

New York ✦ Boston

Little, Brown and Company

Hachette Book Group USA
1271 Avenue of the Americas, New York, NY 10020
Visit our Web site at www.lb-kids.com

First Edition: October 2006

Library of Congress Cataloging-in-Publication Data

Bonk, John J.
  Dustin Grubbs : take two! / John J. Bonk. – 1st ed.
    p. cm.
  Summary: Now in seventh grade, inveterate performer Dustin Grubbs is hoping to star in the school production of *Oliver,* but his father's continuing absence, his aunt's upcoming wedding, a possible role in a national television commercial, and some changes in his long-time friends all make this an especially confusing time for Dustin.
  ISBN-13: 978-0-316-15637-0 (hardcover)
  ISBN-10: 0-316-15637-X (hardcover)
  [1. Theater–Fiction. 2. Fathers–Fiction. 3. Interpersonal relations–Fiction. 4. Family life–Fiction. 5. Schools–Fiction. 6. Humorous stories.] I. Title.
PZ7.B6417Dus 2006
[Fic]–dc22

                                              2006001604

10 9 8 7 6 5 4 3 2 1

Q-FF

Printed in the United States of America

Cover photography by Roger Hagadone
Jacket design by Tracy Shaw
The text was set in Regent, and the display type is Hornpype ITC.

For Chris & Lisa
Writers, resources, friends.

Chapter 1

Missing Pieces

"Dustin, help me find your father's head," Mom said, tossing aside a pair of barbecue tongs. "It's got to be in this box somewhere – buried under all this junk."

I stopped making figure eights on the walls with my flashlight and shone it into the giant box marked DESTROY!

"But, Mom, it's probably all corroded by now."

Our attic was hot and shadowy, and the dim bulb dangling from the ceiling wasn't lighting diddly-squat. Dust specks were floating in the air, never settling anywhere, and the grime was so thick you could taste it. I crouched down and helped my mother dig through Dad's stuff. Dumbbells; record albums – *Vwadek Vushnewski's Polka-Time Favorites* and an entire Jack Benny collection (who?); the coffee-stained Japanese kimono Dad used to wear on weekends; a kazoo.

"There're dust bunnies forming in my nostrils," I

complained. "Are you sure it's in here? I mean, like Principal Futterman says, 'Heads will roll.'"

"I know I put it in that plastic bag – with the others. Keep looking."

Okay, before you start thinking this is going to be some gory tale of murder and suspense, let me set you straight. See, the day my parents separated, which was three years ago and counting, Mom had a fit and crammed everything Dad left behind into the box that the dishwasher came in. He had left us and Buttermilk Falls to chase his dream of becoming a stand-up comedian, which no one found very funny. Then one night after their divorce was official, right in the middle of watching *Family Bliss* (another sitcom with wisecracking kids, a fat husband, and a pretty wife), Mom ripped a large family photo off the wall and cut out Dad's head. Real neat and careful with an X-Acto knife.

She followed that up by going through every photo album in the house on a decapitating rampage. I called it her Lizzie Borden phase. You know, that nutball who whacked off her family's heads with an ax? I'd decided not to hold her accountable for any acts of craziness during that time (Mom – not Lizzie) because I was crazy upset myself, so I could relate. At least Mom had the decency to save all the heads in a Baggie. And she never did destroy that box marked DESTROY!

"I keep telling you, Mom, those Press'n Seal things on the plastic bags never stay closed."

We searched, quiet and sweaty, but weren't making "headway" – and I wasn't able to hold in my burning question for one more second.

"So why the sudden urge to patch things up? You know, with the photos?"

Mom lowered the flashlight and eyeballed the wooden beam next to her as if the answer she was searching for were carved into it somewhere. "Your father keeps joking around about making a surprise visit," she said in a whisper, even though no one else was around. "It's taken us so long to get to the point where we are now –"

"You mean speaking to each other without screaming?"

"Exactly. I'd hate to have him pop in one day only to discover his mug missing in every photo in the house. Especially the big one – he loved that thing."

"Gotcha."

Dad's thinking about showing his face in enemy territory again? And Mom's worried about hurting his feelings if he does? Major progress! Still, I knew not to get too worked up over stuff like that anymore – just in case it backfired.

"Will you help me paste in all the heads later?" she asked.

I nodded. Filling the holes in the photos would be the easy part – filling the hole in my heart was another story.

"If you want, I can scan the smaller pictures into my computer," I told her, "work a little magic, and voilà! – have 'em looking like new."

"Oh, honey, you can do that?" Mom gave my arm a little squeeze. "And I thought twelve-year-olds were supposed to be difficult. I must've hit the jackpot."

"Just remember that thought when Christmastime rolls around."

Mom's flashlight was beginning to poop out so she gave it a good shake. It was one of those cool magnetic-force flashlights that don't use batteries – but you had to rattle it whenever it ran out of juice. The light beam returned and Mom aimed it into the box, which was my cue to get back to the task at hand. I drudged through Dad's baseball cap collection, an old magic kit, hair-in-a-can. . . .

"Hey," I said, lunging for something black and shiny, "what's that?"

"Did you find the head? The big one?"

I dove into the box up to my armpits and came out with a handful of patent leather.

"Tap shoes? *Score!* I didn't know Dad could dance."

"He can't. Believe me." Mom rocked back on her heels, blotting her forehead with her wrist. "He picked those up at a garage sale for a few bucks. Tried them on a few times, and that was the end of that."

"Just one more thing he didn't follow through with, I guess. So can I –?"

"No," she said before I'd even finished. "They're four sizes too big for you. You'll kill yourself."

"I'll stuff 'em. So can I have 'em? Please, please, *please*?"

"I don't want you ripping up my floor with those things."

"You don't understand. I ran into Darlene Deluca at the bookstore yesterday and she swore on a stack of *Teen Vogue*s that we're definitely doing a musical at school this year. Her dance teacher might choreograph. And get this: She told me I'd better get a few *tap* classes under my belt if I knew what was good for me. Talk about fate, right?"

Just as I clapped the shoes onto the floor, a loud *thwap!* came from the other side of the attic. We both jumped.

"What was that?" Mom asked, nervously looking over her shoulder.

"Bats maybe? I remember Granny saying once that we have bats in our belfry."

"I think she said your aunt Birdie has bats in *her* belfry."

It must've been the attic door banging. The sound of *creak-creak-sigh, creak-creak-sigh* was rising up the stairwell, and Aunt Olive eventually appeared in the narrow shaft of light seeping through the window.

"Good Lord, I can't do stairs anymore," she said, all out of breath.

Aunt Olive was a tad on the heavy side. Nothing ridiculous – just a few extra layers of comfort. She was my favorite aunt, but I'd never say it out loud just in case it got back to Aunt Birdie. They both lived downstairs with Granny Grubbs. Mom and I lived in the upstairs apartment with my demon teenage brother, Gordy. Just one big happy family – well, big, anyway.

"I saw the light on from the driveway and said to myself, 'Now's your chance, Olive.'" She grabbed onto a birdcage stand to steady herself, letting out her final huffs and puffs. "I don't like coming up here alone – it gives me the heebie-jeebies."

Mom and I went back to headhunting while my aunt searched through the drawers of an antique dresser that was wedged under the slantiest section of roof. Eventually Mom asked, "Are you looking for something in particular, Olive?"

"Mm-hm."

We waited for the rest of her answer, but none came. "Well, can we shed a little light on the subject for ya?" I offered, meaning the flashlight.

"Oh, that's okay. I just found what I wanted." She closed the drawer with a smack and waved something around in front of her. "It's a silly little nothing – an old lace hanky. I'll bet you don't even know what that is, do you, Dustin?"

"A snot rag. Did you run out of tissues or something?"

My aunt chuckled like that was a joke, but I was really asking.

"Well, I should get an early start on dinner," she said, trotting past us. "Chicken piccata in lemon-caper sauce! I'm learning new recipes – expanding my horizons."

Mom encouraged her with a spunky "Good for you!"

"I just hope it doesn't expand my rear end!" Aunt Olive laughed a musical laugh that could only come out of an ex-opera singer and creaked her way back down the stairs.

Back to making my case. "Speaking of expanding horizons," I said, "remember the standing ovation I got in *The Castle of the Crooked Crowns* at school last May? Well, my public will be expecting even more from me this year, don't ya think?"

"Your public?"

"Everybody already knows acting is my life, but if I'm going to make it in show-biz, I need to develop all my hidden talents. With the musical coming up, tap dancing could be the next step. Hey, good one. *Step* – get it?" She didn't seem to get it – or want it. I twisted up onto my feet and started pacing. "Seriously, Mom," I continued, running a finger through the soot on a dented air conditioner, "what if I'm, like, a natural born tap-dancing genius, only you never let me find out? Can you live with that guilt for the rest of your life?"

"Oh, I think so. We can't afford lessons if that's what you're getting at."

I autographed the air conditioner, then scooped up the tap shoes anyway. They were all cracked and scuffed. And the curly, rotted insoles smelled like – well, no garden of roses, like Granny would say. Still, I knew I had to have them. Maybe they originally belonged to a famous hoofer from the old movie musicals, like Fred Astaire or Gene Kelly. Maybe I was breathing in authentic star stench! I took another whiff and nearly horked up a lung.

"Dustin, what are you doing? Either help me or don't, but stop hovering."

"I'm not hovering, I'm –"

"Here, catch!" Mom said, tossing a deflated football over her head. "Can you use that?"

I watched as it bounced off my chest and flopped onto the grimy floor.

"A football? Mom, have we met?"

"Well, you said you wanted to expand your horizons."

"Not *that* wide." I picked up the pigskin with my fingertips as if it were a dead rat and dropped it back into the box.

Was that supposed to be a subtle hint? Buttermilk Falls was one big sports town, but obviously that wasn't my thing. Gordy's neither. With his numerous ex-girlfriends, I guess you could say he was into "broad-jumping," but that ended when he met his current steady, Rebecca. So Mom was probably spending sleepless nights wondering why. Why was the jock chromosome missing in her two kids?

"We've been over this already. It's not that I don't like sports," I explained, "it's that sports don't like *me*. That doesn't mean I'm weird or anything."

She swept the hair out of her eyes and refueled the flashlight with a double-handed shake.

"But if you think about it, *tap dancing* is kind of a sport," I went on, "only with musical accompaniment and top hats."

"You never let up, do you? All right already, Mr. Relentless, take the darn shoes. Just stick to the backyard when you're wearing them."

"But, Mom, get real – you can't tap-dance on grass."

Not wanting to come off like an ingrate, I thanked her with a peck on the cheek. I was tying the shoelaces together, watching the disco-ball reflections from the shiny taps dancing on the walls, when something fluttered out of one of the shoes and landed down the front of Mom's shirt.

"*Eeesh!*" she yipped, fumbling the flashlight. "What on Earth –?" She plunged a hand down her top, squealing like a mouse in a blender, until she flicked something away with a final scream.

I looked around the floor for a daddy longlegs or worse. Lying in a piddly puddle of light was Dad's mug grinning at me. I plucked it up and examined it more closely. His eyes were crossed. I'd never noticed that before.

"Is this what you're looking for?" I wiggled it in Mom's face.

"Oh, Dustin, you found it!" she gushed.

"Just doing my job, ma'am," I said, sounding like a crime detective who had just cracked a case. "Don't lose your head."

Chapter 2

"Singin' Down the Drain"

I knew it. Tap-dancing on grass was like applauding with mittens on – it just didn't work. And the sidewalk scratched up the taps. To top it off, Ellen Mennopi, my nosy ten-year-old neighbor, was hanging over the fence between our yards giving me the tenth degree. Everybody's called her LMNOP ever since I can remember, but to this day she still thinks we're using her first and last name.

"Are those tap shoes, Dustin Grubbs?"

She called everybody by both names in return.

"Yep."

"With real taps – not just cleats, right?"

"Right."

"Cool. You taking lessons?"

"Nope."

One-syllable answers to annoying questions are extremely satisfying.

Even though it was one of those thick, sticky August nights where the breeze feels like it's coming out of a blow-dryer, I was determined to give my tap shoes a test run. I tip-tapped along the artificial flagstone that bordered the weed garden to see if I could get better sounds. Nope.

"Omigod, know what?" LMNOP said, tumbling off the fence. "There's a coupon in this week's *Penny Pincher*. I think it's for one free class at Miss Pritchard's Academy of Dance – you know, on Main Street? Over the VFW Hall? With all the steamy windows? Darlene Deluca takes classes there. It's supposed to be good."

My ears perked up big-time, but I played it cool. This kid was a blabbermouth, and if there was one thing I'd learned it was to mind my LMNOPs and Qs.

"I can give you the coupon if you want."

"That's okay." I hopped up onto the wooden bench where Granny always played Chinese checkers with who-ever was brave enough to take her on. "I'm just goofin' around."

Besides, we had a copy of the *Penny Pincher* sitting on the radiator in the kitchen and I didn't want to owe LMNOP any favors. *That newspaper rules!* They did a full-page article about me "saving the show" last year. Instant celebrity! I still get recognized on the streets. Well, okay – only in Buttermilk Falls, which is a very small town – where everybody knows every-body. Even so . . .

"You should check it out," LMNOP said over my clattering feet. "You might turn into a triple threat."

"A what?"

"A singing-dancing-acting actor." She popped up a finger for each. "Then you'd have three times the odds of making it in show-biz. But even for an actor-actor, a dance class couldn't hurt."

Triple threat. I liked the sound of that. LMNOP sure knew a lot about a lot – she was very well-rounded for such a bony girl.

"Did you know that NFL football players take ballet classes?"

Then again, she did come out with some pretty off-the-wall stuff. I didn't bother answering, but let my feet do all the talking.

"To improve their coordination and flexibility," Little Miss Know-It-All added.

"Yeah, right." Somehow I couldn't picture those hulking guys in pink shoulder pads with matching tutus.

"No, it's a fact!"

"Well, maybe private lessons . . . in the middle of the night . . . with armed guards at the door," I said. "And definitely *not* at Miss Pritchard's Academy of Dance!"

Having the final word on a subject was even more satisfying than those one-syllable answers. I flew off the bench attempting to do a fancy turn in the air and wound up lying in a heap under the rose trellis on a patch of dead ivy. I think I'd stubbed my entire body.

"You all right, twinkle toes?"

"Don't call me that." I sat rubbing the dirt off my shoes with my thumbs. Part of me wanted to get up and keep tapping, but most of me decided it was time for a breather.

"Sooo," LMNOP lisped over a chorus of crickets, "are you stoked about starting school tomorrow with your new teacher, Mr. Lynch? Do you think he's as strict as they say? Did you know he only wears bow ties?"

"I'm sorry, but this concludes the question-and-answer portion of the evening."

She was rapidly getting on my nerves, so I pulled myself up to my feet and limped toward the house. In the darkness LMNOP looked no wider than a picket.

"Well, I guess I should get my kitty-care-kit ready for your aunt. I'm really gonna miss Cinnamon; she's such a sweetie. Still, I'm *super* excited about my trip tomorrow." I swear, fireflies were zigzagging to dodge the lisp spittle shooting out of her mouth. "So's my dad. He's so psyched, he hasn't slept since Saturday. Seriously."

LMNOP gets to miss the first six weeks of school because she's going with her parents to New England to study endangered whales. Lucky dog! Anyway, my aunt Birdie volunteered to pet-sit her cat while they're away, without clearing it with me first – even though she knows I'm not a big fan of cats. (Notice how you never hear anyone say "lucky cat"?)

"Yep, my dad's finally gonna be living out his fantasy, even if it's just for a little while," LMNOP went on. I was bouncing the screen door open with my rear end, waiting for her to stop yammering. "The only body of water we've got within a fifty-mile radius is Buttermilk Creek, and it's half dried up. That can't be easy for a marine biology professor."

"Talk about a fish out of water! That's as bad as trying to be a stand-up comedian in this town."

"I know, right? Hey, I could send you postcards if you want. Or even e-mail you, like, digital photos of humpbacks – if you're interested."

I didn't answer because that wasn't really a question, even though it sounded like it. To be honest, a complete break from her would be better. Without any pictures of lumpy fish as reminders.

"I'll send postcards. It's not a problem, really."

"Whatever. Okay, I have to take a shower now," I lied, "to beat the morning rush. Have a nice trip."

"G'night, Dustin Grubbs. Don't let the bedbugs bite."

As soon as the screen door slammed behind me, that shower seemed like a good idea for real. After the attic and the yard, I was living up to my name – dusty and grubby.

I stepped into our shower upstairs wearing my swim trunks with the palm trees and coconut design. This was my usual drill ever since Mom accidentally painted over the lock on the bathroom door. See, I was strongly against public displays of nudity (especially my own) and with a bum lock and a crazy family, I wasn't taking any chances. I had lathered, rinsed, and was about to repeat when I got to thinking about fate. First the tap shoes appear; then *abracadabra,* the coupon! First Dad disappears; then, *bibitty-bobitty-boo,* he's back in the picture again. Literally.

I didn't know what the heck was going on, but there was one thing I was suddenly dead sure of: You get *great* tap sounds in the shower! Just bare feet on wet tub. Discovering it was a complete accident, but I couldn't resist belting out "Singin' in the Rain" at the top of my lungs and doing a splashy pretend tap routine. *Stand back, world, I'm a triple threat!* After my showstopping finish, I whipped open the shower curtain to take my bow and –

"Hey!"

My mutant teenage brother, Gordy, was standing there with a camcorder aimed right at me! I went for the curtain again quick, but my feet slipped. Flailing arms . . . fistfuls of slick plastic . . . curtain rings shooting . . .

Yelping!

      Twisting!

            Popping!

                  Falling!

Next thing I know I'm lining the tub, wound in yards of bright yellow vinyl. My horoscope was right: It was proving to be an accident-prone day.

"Are you all right, dweeb?" Gordy reached out to help me with one hand, but kept the camera steady with the other. Oh, yeah – he was busting a gut the whole time.

"*No!* Yes. I'll live." The jerk jerked me to my feet. "It's not funny, freakazoid! I could've cracked my skull and it would've been all your fault."

"You look like a wet banana."

"Turn that thing off," I yelled. "Cut! Cut!" (Don't get me wrong. I'm usually a big ham when it comes to being in front of a camera, but I definitely wasn't ready for my close-up.) "Come on, beat it, loser! I can't stand here forever wrapped in plastic like a salami. I'll get all pruney."

But Gordy, being Gordy, ignored me and sat on the toilet seat, cracking up at the playback on the camcorder. "Dad sent us this thing so we could tape junk like this and send it to him," he said. "I'm just following orders."

"He wants us to capture special family moments – not ugly accidents."

"You *are* an ugly accident."

I hurled the loofah sponge at him, but it veered to the right and skimmed Aunt Birdie's headful of curlers poking through the open door.

"Knock-knock. Are you decent?" she asked breathlessly

with her eyes closed tight. "I ran up as fast as I could. Is everybody all right?"

"Yeah, c'mon in," Gordy said, without looking up. "The more the merrier."

"Are you sure?" Aunt Birdie was peeking through one eye and pumping the top of her polka-dotted housedress for the breeze. "What was that big commotion? I could've sworn I heard Dustin singing and then –"

"You call this singing?" Gordy turned up the volume on the camcorder. "Dustin couldn't carry a tune if it came with handles and a shoulder strap."

Even though I was laminated, I managed to grab the soap-on-a-rope and fling it at Gordy. He flung it right back. Followed by the toilet plunger.

"I told you kids not to play so rough!" Granny growled, shuffling into the bathroom. "And turn down that radio – you'll wake the dead." She was in her flannel nightgown, holding a glass filled with fizzy water and false teeth. "Is Dustin putting on another one of his little skits?"

"No," I muttered, unclogging a waterlogged ear. "And last time I checked you had your own bathroom downstairs. Jeez, can't a guy get a little privacy around here?"

"Man, too bad my thumb got in the way, 'cause this is some killer footage," Gordy said. He turned down the volume on the camcorder, but was still studying the playback on the LCD screen. "Funnier than that stuff they have on that TV show – you know, the one where they dish out big money to losers who send in videotapes of themselves crashing head-first into wedding cakes."

"*America's Goofiest Slips and Trips,*" I offered.

"Yeah."

Aunt Birdie, who'd taken to doing a complete inventory of our medicine cabinet, mumbled something about loving that show. "It's the only TV program that makes me laugh out loud."

"Okay, everybody, party's over," I announced. "Thanks for coming, but mildew is starting to grow under this shower curtain and I really should –"

"Here you all are," a voice said from the hallway.

I could *not* believe it. LMNOP and her big, orange blob of a cat were joining the crowd. *Some nerve!*

"Oh, I don't think so!" I warned, but she barged in anyway.

"Cinnamon just wants to say 'Thank you very much for cat-sitting me, Miss Grubbs,'" LMNOP cooed in a sickening baby voice, bouncing her cat in front of her face like an over-stuffed puppet. "'And I promise to be on my most *purrrfect* behavior.'"

Gag me! Aunt Birdie just encouraged her by shaking its paw and fawning over the thing. "Well, aren't you a sweet kitty boo? Such a fluffy, muffy, scruffy boo."

"Hello!" I snapped. "Teeth chattering. Goose bumps sprouting."

"Alrighty then, I guess I'll see you guys when we get back from Gloucester, Mass.," LMNOP said. "In six weeks or thereabout. And, Dustin Grubbs, I brought you that dance-class coupon just in case. Oh, and you really should give me your e-mail address so I could –"

"*Get out!*" I roared. "*Everybody, ouuut!*"

If this were a scene in a movie, there'd be a reverb sound effect with footage of pigeons flying out of trees and paint curling off walls. Nobody usually listened when I gave orders, but mission accomplished! I had barely begun to unwind myself out of the shower curtain when Gordy barged back in with the camcorder still alive and blinking.

"I'm gonna count to five," I warned through tight lips. "One, one thousand –"

"Don't get your panties in a bunch," he said, setting the camcorder on the hamper. He bent down and scooped up a fingerful of plastic rings from the shaggy rug. "Just lemme help ya get the curtain back up, okay? So Mom doesn't flip out."

"Oh." I switched to my calm voice. "Thanks, Gord."

"Then hop back into the shower, soap up, and we'll take the whole thing from the top!"

Chapter 3

Clean Slate

I was up at the crack, way before my alarm clock went off. But I figured I might as well stay awake and take the extra time getting prepped for my first day as a seventh-grader. Yep, I was now officially an upperclassman. In some towns they're shipped off to a separate school called junior high, but I was still stuck in Buttermilk Falls Elementary – not that big a deal. But big enough. So I splashed on some of Dad's old Aqua Velva aftershave and gelled my hair into a magnificent work of art.

The hordes of kids heading toward school looked like they'd been dipped in new. Unmarked shoes and unmarked notebooks. Clean fingernails, clean slates. And tired old BMF Elementary somehow looked welcoming and full of possibilities. The spotless hallways even smelled like the first day of school – like pressed corduroy and freshly sharpened pencils. And Aqua Velva.

My new teacher sure was a change from my Southern-peach-of-a-teach from sixth grade, Miss Honeywell. His name was Mr. Lynch, and just like LMNOP had reported, he was wearing a bow tie – with red checks. His wrinkled brown suit was loose and crooked (as Aunt Birdie would say, "he was swimming in it") and he had a real pinched-nose-sounding voice. But other than that he seemed all right.

"Welcome to seventh grade," he declared, writing his name across the chalkboard in impossibly perfect cursives. "I know my reputation precedes me, but I'm really not the stick-in-the-mud that some people think. However, I do have a few ground rules. I won't tolerate gum chewing in my class, or foodstuffs of any kind."

Darlene asked if cough drops would be considered "foodstuffs" if they were being used strictly for medicinal purposes. Mr. Lynch seemed thrown, but he okayed it. "There will be no whispering," he droned on, settling at his desk, "no tardiness. And note passing is strictly taboo."

"Did he just say no tattoos?" my best friend, Wally, whispered to me, pulling tiny earphone plugs out of his ears. He'd disappeared for half the summer – it was great knowing I'd see him again on a daily basis.

"No, Wal, but he did say no whispering."

"The young man in the second row with the unkempt hair," Lynch said, snapping his fingers at me. "Button your lip."

"Sorry," I mumbled. *Unkempt? Why, I oughta . . .*

"Now I realize some teachers let their students sit wherever they wish, but I prefer to do it in alphabetical order." He flipped open his long, green ledger. "It's easier that way, so bear with me. When I call out your name, collect your belongings and park yourself at your newly assigned desk. Michael Alvarez . . ."

Wally and I had been sitting next to each other in class since second grade. But if this guy was going to do it in alphabetical order, that meant Wally Dorkin would be nowhere near –

"Dustin Grubbs . . ." Mr. Lynch paused after he got to my name, tugging at his collar. "That name sounds – (gulp) – *familiar*."

Uh-oh, here it comes. The lightbulb going off; the look of horror. I'd been through this routine with every teacher at BMFE.

"You're not *Gordon* Grubbs's brother, are you?"

It's not exactly something you can lie about, but I didn't want him thinking I was a carbon copy of that troublemaker either.

"Only by birth. But don't worry, sir – all we have in common is excessive earwax. It's genetic."

Mr. Lynch closed his eyes and took a deep, cleansing breath. *How could he not know who I am? Does he live under a rock? Didn't he even see the play last year?*

The desk I ended up with was right in the middle of the

third row and had graffiti on it – a bad sketch of a World War II fighter jet bombing a mutant octopus. Plus, hardened glue was filling the pencil groove. *My pencils will be rolling off the desk all year!* Sixteen and a half minutes into seventh grade and I wanted to call it quits.

"Oh, shoot, shoot, shoot!" came from the desk in front of mine. Candice Garboni was frantically digging through her purse and stuff was dropping out everywhere. I waited for Lynch to turn his back before retrieving a tiny jar of goop that had landed on my sneaker.

"My Midnight Madness lip-plumping gloss," she gasped when I handed it to her. "That's what I was looking for!"

Speaking of maturing – Candice, aka Candy, was a girl I'd moved up through the ranks with since first grade, but I hadn't even recognized her until Lynch had assigned her desk. She'd always been quiet and nondescript except for her trademark straight, black hair that hung halfway to the floor. She was still sporting that mane but, *yowza,* the rest of her sure had blossomed over the summer! It was as if she'd been an empty coloring-book outline of herself all those years, and suddenly she was all filled in.

"Thanks, Dust," Candy's shiny mouth muttered as she hung her purse strap over her chair.

"You're welcome. I like your new look. Not everyone can pull off purple lips."

"We can all wait until Mr. Grubbs finishes his conversation,"

Mr. Lynch barked. Candy whipped her head back around so fast, her hair spilled all over my desk. It smelled like fresh strawberries. "That's two strikes against you already. And I believe strike three means you're out."

"That depends if you're talking baseball or bowling."

The class giggled, but Mr. Lynch, obviously having been born without a sense of humor, did not. Still, I gave myself points for coming up with a sports joke.

"All right, ladies and gentlemen," Lynch said, striding over to the chalkboard and grabbing a fat chunk of chalk, "onto our next order of business. On September twenty-third, our class along with Mrs. Sedgwick's eighth-graders will be going on an all-day field trip to the Shedd Aquarium. Truly, truly a fascinating place." There were murmurs of excitement as he wrote the info on the board. Stewy Ziggler was creeping down the aisle, copying every word into his notebook. The kid was no bigger than a popcorn shrimp. "Now we thought it best to send permission slips home with everyone today, because – well, getting them signed and returned on time is usually like pulling teeth. So please get this cemented in your brains, people: no slip, no trip."

I swear, right on the word *trip* somebody tripped Stewy. He landed hard – flat on his face right next to me. The class was in hysterics, but Lynch looked outraged.

"Don't you dare laugh!" he scolded. "Are you okay, Stewart?"

"Fine, sir." Stewy scrambled to his feet and rushed back to

his seat. "Except – uh, I'm having a real problem seeing the board from my desk. Maggie's hair is too poofy."

Rustling filled the air and the class turned around in a single motion to gawk at Maggie Wathom, who'd been assigned the desk in front of Stewy. He was right. It looked as if she'd been struck by lightning in a wind tunnel – while flossing with electrical cords.

"*Eeew,* check out the bad perm!" Candy whispered. "Hello, 1980! I heard her mom's practicing to get her beautician's license and uses Maggie as a guinea pig."

"I can appreciate your dilemma, Stewart," Mr. Lynch said dryly, referring back to his ledger. "Miss Wathom, why don't you switch places with him for today – until we can find a permanent solution."

"A *permanent solution* caused her problem in the first place!" I blurted out.

Why do I do it?

The whole class busted out laughing again, even Maggie. But Mr. Lynch's bow tie was twitching from the surge of anger rushing to his face. Just when I thought he was going to hang me by my thumbs for my outburst, the classroom loudspeaker crackled and burped, and Principal Futterman's voice broke through.

"Welcome back, students! I trust you've all had an exciting summer and are eager to dive headfirst into the three *R*s: reading, writing, and arithmetic."

Mr. Lynch stood at attention staring up at the loudspeaker, as if Futterman was the President of the United States.

"Wait, that's actually only two *R*s. Am I right, Judith?" Futterman mumbled.

"That's right, Dan, because you read it wrong," we heard his secretary say. "It's rithmetic, not arithmetic. It's a time-worn saying."

"*Rithmetic?* That's not even a real word. What kind of example are we setting?"

"With all due respect, next time write your own darn speech!"

You tell him, Judith. I couldn't help cracking up.

"Anyway, students," Futterman said over the sound of crumpling paper, "we've got a super year ahead of us with plenty of exciting things planned. But right now Miss Van Rye, head of the newly sanctioned Arts Committee, is chomping at the bit with some news to share."

"*Good mor –!!*" Miss Van Rye's booming voice rattled the speaker. "Oh, too close? Sorry. How about now? Testing, testing. She sells seashells by the seashore, she sells –"

"While I'm still young," Futterman interrupted.

"Too late," his secretary called out in the background.

"Good morning, munchkins," Miss Van Rye said. "After the smashing success of last year's play, *The Castle of the Crooked Crowns,* it's clear that Buttermilk Fallians are culture-starved and hungry for more, more, more. So this year we have something truly exciting planned: a big, splashy Broadway musical! But that's not all. The Fenton High drama club, woefully overlooked for years, is hitching their wagon to our star. That's right, kiddles – we'll be teaming up for a theatrical extravaganza, the likes of which this town has never seen! Oooh, it's so thrilling I can hardly stand it!"

My thoughts exactly! Darlene's too, I'm guessing – she screamed full out.

"Performances will be at the high school in December, but the jury is still out as to which musical will be chosen. One thing we know for sure: We're going to need plenty of triple threats. So all you supertalents out there, now's your chance to strut your stuff! The sign-up sheet will be posted outside the main office at the beginning of next week. Back to you, Dan – *err*, Principal Futterman."

Microphone fumbling . . . grumbling . . . rumbling. Then back to the Head Honcho.

"On a completely different note, it's our turn to host the Slam-Dunk Basketball Tournament in April. Go, Fireballs!" Futterman cleared his throat. "As some of you may have heard, Claymore Middle School in Lotustown hosted last year and it really put them on the map. But I think we'll be rubbing their noses in it when they get a load of the brand-spanking new Mascot 2000 digital scoreboard that's just been delivered to our gymnasium."

All the jocks in the room cheered for that news flash.

"However, due to some minor cutbacks, the new uniforms that were promised have now been scrapped."

The cheering went sour and Danny "Pig" Piglowitz lined a spitball at the loudspeaker.

"Apparently theatrical extravaganzas don't come cheap," Futterman added. "My hands are tied, guys, but believe me, if I had my druthers . . ."

Buzz. Burp. Click.

Chapter 4

No Small Feat

What are druthers and how come nobody ever has any? I'd planned on looking that word up in the dictionary right after "triple threat." I wanted to make sure I had the meaning exactly right, but according to *The American Heritage Dictionary,* fourth edition, it didn't exist. They had Triple Crown, triple-header, triple play – but no triple threat. I'd just have to take LMNOP's word for it. My acting chops were solid, but singing and dancing was uncharted territory, so I knew I'd better get cracking.

All week long I toyed with the idea of cashing in one of my *Penny Pincher* coupons and taking a free tap class; and all week long the thought of being the only guy there made me squirrelly. But by Saturday morning, I'd talked myself into it. I carbo-loaded with leftover Meatball Mania Pizza, stuffed Dad's tap shoes into my backpack, mounted my bike and headed for Miss Pritchard's Academy of Dance.

I'd reached the center of town way too early, where I saw the screwballiest sight: Wally squeaking down Main Street on a girl's bicycle, complete with a white wicker basket and handgrips sprouting silver streamers. A cry for help maybe? You be the judge.

"Hey, Wal, wait up!" Pedaling faster to catch up with him, I had a sudden stroke of genius. "What're you doing right now?"

"Juggling chickens. What does it look like I'm doing?"

"Race you to the corner?" I challenged, air-revving my hand-grips. "*Vroom-vroom, vroom-vroom!* C'mon, winner gets a truth or dare."

He looked at me as if *I* were the weirdo.

"What are we, like, five?" Wally asked. "You serious?"

"Yeah. Why not?

"Well, for starters, I'm lugging my bassoon and it weighs a ton. And this isn't even my own bike – it's my cousin's."

"Now that you mention it, what the heck's wrong with you? Goldilocks wouldn't be caught dead riding that thing."

"My bike has a flat," he snapped, "and I needed trans-portation. Cut me a break."

At least it didn't have training wheels.

"Okay, I'll give you a five second lead so I won't have an unfair advantage," I bargained. "Ready? One Mississippi, two Mississippi –"

"No, no, that's not right," Wally said all cranky, dragging his foot. "I'll take a *twelve* second lead – and we're not playing hide-and-seek. There are no Mississippis in bike-race counting."

"There's no whining either."

"Okay, first one to slap the mailbox on the corner of Cubberly and Main wins. On your mark, get set, go!" As soon as he had both feet on the pedals, I shouted, "One, two, three-four-fi-si-sev-eigh-nitenelev-*twelve!*" and tore after him.

I was on his tail in a flash, and by the time we'd reached Pig's Ear Antiques, Wally and I were neck and neck. I could hear him moaning and his bassoon case rattling, so I coasted a little. He was thicker around the middle than he should've been and I didn't want him straining anything. All of a sudden he turned to me and snarled, "You're goin' down, sucker!"

"Oh, yeah?" I shot back. "Eat my dust!"

I stood up on my pedals, throwing all seventy-six and a half pounds of myself into it. Picturing my legs as powerful steel machines operated by jet propulsion engines, I whizzed past Wally and headed for the finish line. I was pedaling so hard I thought my bike would break in half.

"Woo-hoo!" I shouted, slapping the mailbox. "Dustin Grubbs wins it by a landslide!" No wonder so many kids love sports. It's actually kind of exhilarating – as long as you win. "Sweet victory! I am the conqueror, the annihilator! Oh, how the mighty have fallen!"

Wally squeezed on the brakes and his bike came to a jerky stop. "Ah, get over yourself," he huffed. His red cheeks were streaked with sweat. "Okay, you won, big whoop – you set me up. Let's make a pact never to do this again, okay? The carbuncle on my thigh is on fire."

I didn't have a clue what that was, and I didn't want to know.

"So what's it gonna be," I asked, "truth or dare?"

"Dare." He studied the expression on my face while he untwisted his bassoon case strap. "No, truth! No, wait – scratch that. Okay, dare."

"Excellent choice." *Saves me having to trick him into it.* "Let's see. Dare-dare-dare-dare . . ." I paused as if I were browsing a menu of dares in my head. "Okay, I dare you, Wallace P. Dorkin, to take a tap class with me at Miss Pritchard's Academy of Dance."

"Not a chance! Never gonna happen. Besides, you're supposed to give me a dare I could do right now, like swallow a bug or something."

"It *is* right now." I glanced at my watch. "In ten minutes. And you don't even need tap shoes – just hard-soled shoes, like the ones you're wearing. I called and asked."

"I'm meeting up with some band-camp friends."

Band-camp friends. Those words were like three poison darts to the chest.

"I told you," he said, retucking the rumpled mess he called a shirt, "as soon as I can snag a semidecent French horn player I'm forming a woodwind quintet. I still don't get why Mozart and Bach and those guys stuck a brass instrument in with a bunch of woodwinds when they wrote their chamber music, but . . ."

I didn't understand half the words spilling out of Wally's mouth. While he was blabbering away I did a double take. Some guy kept running up and down the steps of the library across the street.

"Hey, Wal, check out that nut job," I said snickering. "He doesn't know whether he's coming or going."

"That's no nut job." Wally was craning his neck to see past a Lotustown bus. "That's that eighth-grader, Zack Kincaid, captain of the Fireballs. The hulky guy standing there with the stopwatch is his father – supposed to be a real jerk."

"What do you think they're doing?"

"Training. His dad wants Zack to get athletic scholarships, so he's always cracking the whip."

"How do you know that?" I asked.

"How do you *not* know that?"

We hopped onto our bikes and began pedaling down Main Street in silence. Well, except for Mr. Kincaid's distant "Hustle! Hustle!" and the Walrus groaning about his burning carbuncle.

"There's another beginning tap class on Wednesday night," I said, back to the subject at hand. "How about that one? I'll treat you to a swirl cone after. Large."

"No can do, my friend."

"C'mon, man! What if I'm, like, the only boy there?"

"So? Don't go – no one's twisting your arm." Wally sounded annoyed and I could feel the fight in me petering out. "Ask Pepper to go with you."

"Pepper's not a boy."

"Half the people in Buttermilk Falls think she is."

"Nice talk," I said, shaking my head.

"Don't tell her I said that."

I decided to drop the subject of the tap class completely. Didn't want to spark one of our epic grudgefests. They can get ugly.

"Well, wish me luck, Wal," I said, jumping the curb in front of the dance studio. "Call me later, okay?"

"You call *me*."

"No, *you* call me!"

Miss Pritchard's Academy of Dance was up a steep, narrow stairway. I cashed in my coupon with a lady at the front desk who directed me through a hallway of noisy little girls to the boys' changing room. No big surprise that it was dark and deserted. I was nervously changing into Dad's tap shoes, which were prestuffed with socks for a better fit, when I heard "Class is starting! Let's go, girls! And *boy*."

Thanks for that.

Two seconds later, I was standing in a mirror-covered room, white-knuckling a long, wooden bar alongside the wall.

Looking down the lineup of little bunned heads on either side of me, I was tempted to make a run for it. But on the bright side I did feel extremely tall.

"Well, look who showed!" Darlene Deluca said, sneaking up on me. "You've got guts – I'll give you that much. But you always did like standing out in a crowd."

"Oh, hi, Darlene." Did I mention she was the bossiest girl at Buttermilk Falls Elementary? Possibly the entire Midwest? "I didn't think you'd be in the beginners class."

"As if!" she exclaimed, and bent over to buckle her tap shoes – without even bending her knees. "How pathetic would that be after studying for three and a half years? I'm the TA, as in teacher's assistant. I get paid for it too, as in money."

"Uh-huh," I said, as in who cares?

"I'm only covering the tap classes so far, but –?" Darlene got a load of my tap shoes and fell into a sudden fit of laughter. "Omigod, where'd you find those things? They're gigantic! Do they explode?"

The giggles that were spreading across the room from girl to girl came to an abrupt stop when the woman from the front desk floated into the room wearing all black. Probably Miss Pritchard. She was short and spunky – the type of adult you'd swear was a teenager if her face were covered in zits instead of wrinkles.

"Okay class, we're going to begin with our usual warm-up," she announced, as Darlene flew to her side. "And for the new boy, just follow along as best you can. You'll catch on."

Famous last words.

"Darlene, whenever you're ready."

Darlene grabbed a small drum off the piano and started beating it with a steady *boom-boom-boom,* like a human metronome. Miss Pritchard matched the beat, chanting, "Flap-heel, flap-heel, flap-flap, shuffle-ball-change . . ." Everybody knew *exactly* what they were doing, but I didn't know a flap from a flapjack.

"I thought this was supposed to be beginning," I moaned to the girl in front of me.

"Beginning level three."

"Heads up!" Miss Pritchard barked. "You, the new boy – head up! Loose knees, everyone – stay in *demi plié.* Good. Shoulders back. Keep a slight *relevé.*"

"Why is she speaking in foreign tongues?" I whispered to the same nibblet of a girl. She was wearing head-to-toe pink, and her tights were anything but tight.

"It's French. *Relevé* means –"

"No talking!" Miss Pritchard yelled. The little pink girl bit her lip.

Except for the language barrier, I made it through all the warm-ups thinking *so-far-so-good* thoughts. Then we started doing turns across the floor. In my opinion, they were way too tough for beginning level three – or four or five! During our second go-round, I was whirling out of control like a spastic top, thinking up possible excuses for a quick exit. Sprained ankle? Important phone call? Jock itch?

"The new boy!" Miss Pritchard called out. I came to a standstill, causing a tapping train wreck. "You're going to get dizzy if you don't spot."

Too late. My head was still spinning even though my body had stopped.

"Pick a spot on that far wall," Miss Pritchard instructed, "and every time you whip your head around, your eyes return to that very same spot. Darlene, please demonstrate."

Darlene stuck her nose in the air and spun across the floor like a ballerina on fast-forward. I did my best to copy her, but ended up in a heap on the floor. The bun brigade got a big kick out of that.

"Well, no wonder you're tripping all over yourself," Miss Pritchard said as I scrambled to my feet. "I'm surprised you can even *walk* in those shoes, let alone dance! I'll tell you what. Go dig through that green canvas bag under the window and find yourself a pair of tap shoes that fit."

There was only one boys' pair at the bottom of the bag, and they were missing a heel tap, but anything would've been an improvement. So I quickly changed into them and set Dad's tap shoes on the windowsill before rejoining the line of twirling tots. Then I tried – boy, how I tried – with every fiber of my being, to "spot" the lousy clock on the wall. But with each turn it got fuzzier and I got dizzier, while the meatballs in my stomach were being whipped into a frothy frappe. *Gawd, I really stink at this and I can't even blame Dad's clown shoes anymore!* I kept tapping . . . turning . . . with my insides thrashing . . . churning – until I yelled, "Clear the way!" and spun myself right out the door.

I staggered down the hall, ricocheting off the walls and aiming for the boys' changing room. *I don't remember if there was a sink in there. Or even a toilet!* Plunging into the dark room, I desperately felt around the doorjamb searching for the light switch. A wave of nausea was boiling up inside me like molten lava. And just as I switched on the light, my volcano erupted and liquid meatballs came spewing out my mouth.

"*Blaaargh!*"

"Hey!" someone screeched, and I felt a powerful shove.

I went flying across the room and slammed my knees into the long bench, not knowing what had hit me. A second eruption was on its way – but the stinging pain from my broken kneecaps and dislocated shoulder must've stopped it from coming. Collapsing onto the bench, I turned to see a hysterical guy jumping around in front of me with road pizza all over his sneakers.

"Jeez! Idiot! Freakin' idiot!"

"Sorry!" I said, wiping my sour mouth. "Gawd! I didn't know anyone was even in here!"

I limped over to the sink – it turns out there *was* a sink – grabbed a bunch of paper towels and hobbled back to clean up the mess on the floor.

"Don't come near me, wuss!" the kid growled all bug-eyed. "Just back away. Far away."

"Okay, okay!"

I dropped the towels into the puddle and gave him room. While I was frantically changing back into my street shoes, the kid kept pacing back and forth, trying to shake the stuff off his feet. He looked familiar. Tall and gangly; buzz cut; skin so white you could see through it. I was pretty sure it was that Zack guy who we just saw racing up and down the library steps. What were the odds? And why was he hiding out in the dark dressing room of Miss Pritchard's Academy of Dance? Must've been picking up his little sister from class or something.

"Again, I'm really, *really* sorry."

He let out a cry of anguish and punched a locker before escaping into the hall. I quickly shoved my stuff into my backpack and rushed out after him, bumping right into Miss Pritchard. "Ooh, sorry!"

"What's going on?"

"Accident," I said, hustling past her. "Should I – do you want me to –?"

She palmed her forehead when the smell hit her and I think she started cursing in French. "Darlene!" she bellowed.

"Protein spill in the boys' dressing room. Bring the mop quick!"

"Oh, great!" I heard Darlene yell from the classroom as I was hightailing it toward the exit. "Boys wreck everything!"

Halfway down the steps I realized that Dad's tap shoes were still sitting on the windowsill. Halfway up, I decided they'd just have to stay there because I was never going back.

Chapter 5

Triple Threat

Before the weekend had run out, I'd come to the conclusion that becoming a *double* threat rather than a triple threat wouldn't be the worst thing in the world. I mean it was painfully obvious that I wasn't exactly blessed with the gift of dance. Just ask Zack Kincaid's shoes.

On my way out of school on Monday, right after the final bell, Miss Van Rye stopped me and asked if I'd give her a hand. I turned and applauded. Not something you can pull with every teacher, but she ate it up. She cackled and did a sort of grand diva curtsy, then told me to follow her. Even though she'd been a kindergarten teacher most of her life, telltale signs of her brief stint as a young actress in New York always bled through.

"Where're we going?"

"The storage room. To see if any scenery from *The Castle of the Crooked Crowns* is salvageable."

"I'm surprised they even kept it," I said, practically skipping down the corridor. She was an extremely fast walker for a teacher of such epic proportions. "Isn't it in pretty bad shape?"

"One can only hope."

"Huh?"

"If anyone asks, I never said that. See, the high school doesn't have much at all to work with scenery-wise. So if ours is in ruins, it looks like we'll be –" She stopped short and grabbed both my hands. Her eyeballs were dancing. "We'll be renting professional sets for the show! Isn't that thrilling?"

"Omigod, that's fantastic!" And we were off again – her brightly-colored caftan billowing in the breeze.

"The Arts Committee did the math and realized it wouldn't cost much more than if we had to build it ourselves from scratch. And Lord only knows what it'd turn out like. Anyway, don't get too excited just yet. It all hinges on what we find in storage."

The thought of performing in a musical with professional sets had me so pumped up, I paid little attention to the shouts and whistle blasts echoing through the corridor.

"So have you guys decided what show we're gonna do?" I figured I'd take advantage of our face time and squeeze all the info out of her I could get.

"We have indeed. But I'm not supposed to spill the beans

just yet. The sign-up sheet will be posted tomorrow and you'll know then."

All I ask is that Darlene was wrong, and it doesn't end up being some heavy tap show like Forty-Second Street. *And of course there has to be a juicy part in it for me!*

We hustled down the hall and the sound of squeaky sneakers on highly polished floors was getting louder and louder. After three o'clock that could only mean one thing: the basketball team was rehearsing – practicing, I mean, and the gymnasium doors were left open. Miss Van Rye led me through them, straight into enemy territory. *Why?*

"Yoo-hoo, Lou?" Miss Van Rye called out, waving to the coach. "I'm so sorry to interrupt, but may I borrow your keys to the storage unit?"

Oh, that's right – after our show had closed, we'd broken down the set and stored it inside the gym behind the green, padlocked door. Phys ed classes were bad enough; I always steered clear of that place unless absolutely necessary.

"In my office. Top drawer of my desk," Coach Mockler hollered. He seemed peeved – barely took his eyes off the basketball game in progress. Miss Van Rye left me stranded and scurried around the outskirts of the gym, heading toward the locker rooms. She almost bumped into the gi-normous scoreboard, which was half-covered in bubble wrap, leaning against the wall.

"If it's not there, try the black filing cabinet. Or the closet. Or my gym bag."

This could take days. I took off my backpack and hovered near the door, pretending to be engrossed in the game (like that would ever happen). In reality I was grossed out by the smell of sweat. It was intense, like hot chicken soup.

"Are you here to try out?" Mockler asked. I whipped my head around, thinking someone else was behind me. "Yeah, Grubbs, I'm talking to you!" The Fireballs were still in the heat of their game, but some laughed right out loud.

"Oh, no, sir. I'm just helping Miss Van Rye."

"Everybody makes the team, you know."

"That's okay. I'm good."

He was either pullin' my leg or he'd lost his mind. I slipped back into the hall and pointed my astonished expression to the trophy display case hanging on the wall. I'd never realized how many trophies and plaques our sports teams had racked up over the years. Right in the middle of all that hardware was a framed newspaper clipping of Shatzi, our principal's mutant-looking dog who served as mascot. According to the article, Mr. Futterman had shaved a big *F* into the poor dog's back for the final game last season. *F* for Fireballs. Probably a little for Futterman too.

A sharp whistle blast made me flinch. "Tyler, whaddya doin'?" Mockler yelled. I peeked into the gym and saw two kids tumbling to the floor in a tangled lump. Heck, even I knew tackling wasn't allowed in basketball. "Why weren't you looking up at the basket? It's like you're in la-la land out there. And Piglowitz, you're playin' like my grandmother." More with the whistle. "All right, guys, time for a little Basketball One-Oh-One."

The boys were gathering around the coach and I immediately spotted beanpole Zack, a head above the rest. He was taking a hit off a bottle of breath freshener – or maybe an asthma inhaler? He noticed me too but wouldn't look directly at me, like I was the sun or something. I wanted to bolt.

"Even though we have a no-cuts policy, remember, only thirteen get to play. So listen up, 'cause it's time to separate the men from the boys." The team was hanging on the coach's every word. "Who can tell me what a triple threat is?"

Did he just say triple threat or are my ears hallucinating? That lured me back inside. Now *I* was hanging on his every word.

"Come on, guys, you know this. In a triple threat stance the offensive player has three different moves he can make: Shoot. Dribble. Or pass."

It's a good thing I'd stopped myself. I'd almost raised my hand and said, "An actor-singer-dancer, like Fred Astaire or Catherine Zeta-Jones."

"Kincaid, you're up! Front and center. Show 'em how it's done."

Zack flew to the middle of the floor and the coach shot him the ball. He caught it like a pro (I'm guessing) and froze in a squat position, holding the ball as if he were about to throw it through the hoop thing – the net thing – the basket.

"Feet shoulder-width apart," Mockler instructed, walking a circle around Zack, "legs slightly bent, back straight, head up."

It sounded exactly like the drill in Miss Pritchard's dance class. *If the jocks start doing turns across the floor I'll wet myself!*

"Good job, Kincaid, but stay low. Keep it tight and don't palm the ball."

"Found 'em, Lou!" Miss Van Rye called out, trotting across the floor with a jumble of keys jingling in her hand. *Jeez, it's about time.* "Which key is it, do you know?" Mockler just grunted. "Oh, never mind, I'll find it. I'm not even here." She took me by the hand like one of her kindergartners and led me to the storage unit at the far side of the gym. "You're such a doll for waiting. You wouldn't believe the disgusting things I had to dig through to find these keys."

Her trial-and-error process took forever. When she finally undid the padlock, I checked to see if my first pair of sideburns had grown in.

"Heavens to Betsy, it's a pigsty in here." Miss Van Rye was having a hard time squishing through the door – I had to give her a slight push. "Yeah, no . . . no . . . no," she muttered, picking through things, "this won't do at all." Reminders of my stellar theatrical debut lay all around us in a disheveled heap. "Refresh my memory – what did we do for costumes last year?"

"Everybody was responsible for their own. Pepper's was a sheet. Mine was a pillowcase."

"Well, that's not going to help – unless we do *Once Upon a Mattress*!" She let out another cackle that ended in a dusty cough. We kept hunting around, but weren't coming up with much. "Yeah, no ... no ... no. Honey, you want to climb back in that corner and see if there's anything other than –"

"Kindling?" I maneuvered my way over a busted drawbridge, muttering, "Yeah, no ... no ... no."

"What's in those boxes, Dustin?"

I started searching through box after filthy box. "Christmas decorations," I reported, "*more* Christmas – oh, wait, here's one marked COSTUME PIECES AND PROPS." I checked inside, but all I found were "Two dented crowns, a rubber chicken, and – *argh!* – a dead mouse!"

We emerged back into the gym with nothing but dangling cobwebs just as two big, burly men in brown jumpsuits came trudging through the gymnasium doors. One was pushing a large, steel dolly.

"Excuse me," he garbled. "You Coach Mockler?"

"Who wants to know?"

"We're from Trektronics – here to pick up the Mascot 2000."

There were a few seconds of silence during which all the Fireballs looked stunned. One, one thousand, two, one thousand. . . . Then in a flash they transformed into an angry mob, closing in on the coach and bombarding him with questions.

"Settle down," Mockler grumbled. He shoved the basketball under one arm and signed the papers on the clipboard that the Treky guy held out. "I don't know why I was holding off telling you boys about this – I guess I was praying for a miracle or something. The scoreboard's gotta go back."

"No way!" Zack cried out. "Why?"

"From what I understand, it never should've have been ordered in the first place." He gestured over to the scoreboard, mumbling, "That's it over there, guys. Help yourselves."

"Uh, we got a problem here, Coach," the burliest guy said over a chorus of hisses and groans. "That thing's supposed to be packed and ready to go."

Mockler slammed the basketball into the bleachers. "Zack, Tyler, Piglowitz, lend us a hand, will ya? The rest of you boys are on a short time-out."

"Isn't that just a doggone shame," Miss Van Rye whispered, meaning the scene that had just played out in front of us. I shrugged. While she was doing up the padlock on the storage room door, Darlene and Maggie sprang out of the girls' locker room and came sprinting over to us, carrying chewed-up-looking pom-poms – more like just poms.

"We're trying out for cheerleader this year and we get to take these things home to rehearse!" Darlene spouted, like anyone asked. "So what're you doing here, barf-breath?" She had the nerve to shake her ratty pom-poms in my face.

"Knock it off! Who invited you?"

"What's going on, Miss Van Rye?" Maggie asked.

"Oh, hello, girls." She jiggled the door to make sure it was locked and turned around smiling. "I was just about to tell Dustin the good news."

"What good news?" Darlene said, bouncing around as if she had squirrels in her pants.

"Well, kids . . ." Miss Van Rye took a dramatic pause like an actress on a soap opera – then bellowed at the top of her lungs, "It looks like we're going to be renting professional sets *and* costumes for our musical!"

"Woo-hoo!" the three of us exploded altogether. *Costumes too! We're really going all out.* Darlene and Maggie were jumping up and down, shaking their pom-poms. Inside myself I was doing the same. Even Miss Van Rye let a girlish squeal slip out.

"I'm sure the Arts Committee will back me up on my decision," she cried, clapping soot off her hands. "So we can just dump that old scenery from last year!"

"Burn it!" Darlene cried out over Maggie's "Who needs it?" Cheers and high fives all around.

"Good riddance!" I yelled through cupped hands as the scoreboard on the dolly went *squeak-squeak-squeaking* out the door.

After the dust settled (I'm talking real dust) and I was strapping on my backpack, I realized there was a gym-full of Fireballs and a red-faced coach scowling at us. I wasn't sure why at first, but then it hit me:

Drama geeks cheering + scoreboard exiting = really bad timing!

Chapter 6

Food for Thought

It was official. As Miss Van Rye had promised, a sign-up sheet was hanging on the bulletin board outside the main office on Tuesday morning. I was afraid to look at first, but as it turned out, Darlene was way off – either that or she had flat-out lied to my face, because *Oliver!* was the show of choice! *Excellent!* I'd seen two different movie versions of it and knew all the characters inside and out. Orphans, pickpockets, upper-crust British well-to-dos. And not a tap-dancer in the bunch. Around tenish, about a dozen names were on the list – as well as a SPORTS RULE! bumper sticker. And come lunchtime, kids were all over that piece of paper like ants on a fumbled ice cream cone. Mostly girls, though. Okay, *all* girls – and me. Story of my life lately.

"So did you sign up to audition?" Wally asked, as we joined the parade of orange plastic trays in the lunch line.

"Do boxer briefs ride up? Dumb question." The cafeteria

lady handed me a warm plate with a toppling sloppy joe on it, and I set it onto my tray. "I thought they'd go for more of a fluff musical, but *Oliver!* has real depth! And I was born to play the Artful Dodger, don't you think?" I didn't wait for his answer. "I mean it's pretty obvious the Arts Committee had that in mind when they made their choice."

"Don't break your arm patting yourself on the back, conceited."

Wally asked the cafeteria lady for an extra helping, which was his usual drill, and we inched our trays along the metal ledge. He was lugging his bassoon in its beat-up leather case, knocking into everything as usual. It always looked like he was going on vacation – especially when he wore his Hawaiian pineapple shirt.

"Hey, don't you have to be able to sing to be in a musical?" Wally asked, ogling the desserts.

"So? What are you getting at?"

"I don't think I've ever heard you sing. Except 'The Star Spangled Banner' with everybody else."

"I sing plenty." Mostly in the shower, but I wasn't coming clean – so to speak.

By the time we'd reached the cash register, our meals were complete with mashed potatoes doused in gray gravy, watery creamed corn, a square of lime Jell-O, and the usual chocolate milk. I grabbed a butter cookie at the last second and added it to my bill. They were expensive at seventy-five cents a piece, but impossible to resist. Wally and I took a seat next to Pepper, who was brown-bagging it at our usual table next to the window. It was pouring rain outside, so the lunchroom was darker and stickier than usual.

"Hey, Wal, are you gonna audition too? You should."

"Nah, been there, done that. Maybe for the orchestra, if there's an orchestra. Do you think they'll have an orchestra?"

I shrugged. "They'll probably use all high school kids."

"You guys talking about the tryouts?" Pepper asked. She was rotating her egg salad sandwich and licking around the edges.

"Auditions, Pep," I said. "Tryouts are for basketball teams. You going?"

"Nah, I'm still recovering from last year's show. Maybe I'll do tech."

A squeal came from a table across the room, where the seventh- and eighth-grade cool girls sat. The Geyser Girls we called them because they were always gushing about every little thing. I didn't pay much attention until I realized that Candy Garboni was the loudest squealer. Zack was lining paper airplanes at her from the next table and they were sticking in her hair. The back of her head looked like an airport tarmac.

"Where does that Zack kid get off?" I said to the others.

"Just 'cause he's king of the jocks doesn't mean he can go around torturing innocent seventh-graders. Do you think I should say something?"

Wally checked out the scene. "Only if you want a bloody lip."

"Ah, leave those two alone," Pepper said, still working on the rim of her sandwich. "It's obviously just puppy love."

"If that's the case, Zack needs to be neutered!" Egg guck shot out of Pepper's mouth from laughing at my zinger. "Thanks for coming, ladies and gentlemen," I said into my microphone-thumb, as if I were winding up a comedy routine, "and enjoy the steak."

"There's steak?" Wally asked.

Candy squealed again, and not in a good way. Tyler and Pig, two Fireballs from my class, had joined in on the Zack-attack. Even though any of them could pound me into mulch with one hand tied behind their backs, I grabbed my cookie and headed for the jock table, unsure of what I was going to do or say.

"It was nice knowing you," Wally called out after me.

I approached the testosterone zone looking easy and breezy. "Hi, guys," I said in my friendliest voice. "Sorry about your scoreboard and everything. Total bummer." Felix Plunket was the only one at the table who bothered looking up at me. Nice kid, Felix.

"Incoming enemy *hair*craft," Zack said, shooting another

plane at Candy. Pig snorted and high-fived Zack for coming up with that little gem.

"Hey, Zack." I knocked on the table. "Zack?"

Finally he turned to me. From the look on his face you'd think I was dripping in raw sewage.

"Don't worry, I'm not gonna blow chunks. I come bearing gifts. Well, gift." I set the cookie on the napkin in front of him. "Think of it as a peace offering for what happened on Saturday at Miss Pritch –"

He cut me off with, "Yeah, whatever."

It suddenly hit me what a brilliant move this was on my part. Creating a diversion to save Candy *and* apologizing for the dance studio incident at the same time. I'm telling you, nobody could resist those butter cookies. When they're baking everyday at around ten-thirty, their sugary scent wafts through the halls, invading unsuspecting nostrils, until the whole school is salivating. No wonder they jacked up the price.

"Fresh out of the oven," I said temptingly. "Still warm. The edges are a crisp golden brown for the perfect amount of crunch. A little taste of heaven." Zack was staring a hole through the cookie and I heard him swallow hard. "See how perfectly round this one is? And a lot bigger than normal."

"Yeah," Zack snarled, "like your head." He crushed the cookie with his fist, grinding it into dust. A crash of thunder rattled the windows. My insides were rattling too, but on the outside I was cucumber cool.

"Well, alrighty then." I backed away slowly. "Some people prefer dunking them in milk, but whatever floats your boat. You folks have a nice day."

Felix gave me a half-wave and I moseyed back to my table.

"Great. Now you're on Zack's hit list," Wally scolded as I slid back into my chair.

"I think I already was."

"You must have a death wish or something. Either that or –" Wally gasped, as if he'd found the answer spelled out in his creamed corn. "You're in love with Candy Garboni!"

"Uh, try again. Not even close, my friend."

Okay, maybe there was a minor fascination there, but nothing worth admitting out loud. When I glanced back at the Geyser Girls, Candy was brushing a fleet of airplanes out of her hair, smiling away like it didn't even bother her.

"Look at her, poor kid – putting on a brave front."

"Gawd, Dust, you are clueless," Pepper said, glaring at Candy. "I'm tellin' ya, she's in hog heaven." I shook my head in disagreement. "Everybody's talking about how she's gone from 'drab to fab' over the summer, but I honestly don't get what the big deal is. I mean did you ever see her up close? She's very hairy."

"Pepper, you're a girl, right?" Wally asked.

"Pretty much."

"Why do girls always fall for jocks?"

"Well, not all girls do – just most." Pepper took a cut-up orange out of a plastic bag and handed a quarter each to Wally and me. "Especially if the guy's hot. Personally, I prefer the sensitive, artistic type. I happen to think Zack is a total dirtbag."

"Ditto," Darlene said, sweeping up to our table. No one even saw her coming – like the measles. "Here, Pepper, you're gonna wanna sign this. Wipe your hands first, though, so you don't muck it up." She slapped a piece of notebook paper in front of Pepper.

"What is it?" Pepper was busy licking her fingers.

"A petition," Darlene replied, "for us to do *Annie* instead of *Oliver!* It's obvious the Arts Committee has a thing for orphans, right? Well, *Annie* is crawling with them, and it's a ten-times better show for a school to do than boring *Oliver!*"

"Ah, your ponytail's pulled too tight," I said, sucking away on my orange wedge. "A musical based on an old, dead comic strip is more educational than a Dickens classic? Fess up. You just wanna play Annie."

"Oh, butt out, butt face," Darlene snapped, "nobody asked you to sign." I flashed her a citrusy smile, with orange peel covering my teeth. "It just makes better sense. There're hardly any female roles in *Oliver!* – and no boys have even signed up to audition for it yet. Except one weirdo."

"Hey!" I shouted.

Darlene bit the cap off her pen and handed it to Pepper. "There's no tap dancing in it, either, Dustin-bin. So it looks like you totally humiliated yourself for nothing at Miss Pritchard's. Ha! Too bad, so sad."

"Which you totally lied to me about," I snapped, staring her in the face. "What the heck's wrong with you? Who would do a thing like that?"

"Listen, the more kids we pack into the tap classes, the more I get paid. It's called being resourceful."

"Well, that was a slimy thing to –"

"Live with it. C'mon, Pepper," Darlene whined, "you're holding me up. Are you gonna sign or not?"

"Don't rush me. Umm ... uhhh ..." Pepper was twirling the pen through her fingers; then positioned it on the paper as if she were going to sign. "*Not!*" she said, tossing the pen into the air.

"Fine! Who needs you?"

Darlene retrieved the pen and the petition, and stomped over to the Geyser Girl table. I strained to hear what she was yammering about, but couldn't really hear much until: "I just wasted five minutes of my lunch hour on a certain redheaded girl with a Y chromosome. Oops! My mistake."

"That's it. She's toast!" Pepper lurched out of her chair with a screech, but I pulled her back down.

"No, don't."

A stream of heavy rain suddenly pelted against the windows, sounding like machine-gun fire as the chatter from across the aisle got louder and louder. It was as if the fury of the downpour was stirring things up in the cafeteria. Zack was sticking his nose in the situation now too, peering over Candy's shoulder and making fun of the whole petition idea. "You guys can't sign this thing," he proclaimed.

Candy asked, "Why not?"

"Who cares *which* lame puppet show the Arts Committee wants to put on? Coach Mockler says they're dipping into the phys ed budget in order to do it."

"That's bogus." Darlene's hand flew to her hip. "Why would they need jock money? Think about it, genius. Fact: *The Castle of the Crooked Crowns* was a big, fat hit. Fact: It earned more profits than all the PTA bake sales and candy drives for the last three years combined."

"Yeah, and this time Fenton High's pitching in," Maggie added, sauntering up to their table, picking at a cupcake. "It's about time us thespians got a little attention."

"Thespians!" Tyler spouted, elbowing Pig. "I can't believe she came right out and admitted it."

"You're an idiot!" Maggie snapped.

I kept feeding my face like it was best lunch ever, but I really was eavesdropping. I could tell Pepper was doing the same. Hard to tell with the Walrus, though.

"Well – er, but," Zack was sputtering, "the school shouldn't have reneged on their promises to the Fireballs. How's it gonna look? Us hosting the Slam-Dunk Basketball Tourney without a freakin' scoreboard?"

"Well, boo hoo for you, Betty Sue." Darlene made a pouty face and mimed drying pretend tears. Maggie laughed outright, but Zack looked steamed. You could practically see flames shooting from his eyes, like the ones on his Fireballs sweatshirt.

"Where's your team loyalty?" he yelled in Darlene's face. "I thought you guys wanna be cheerleaders!"

"Not anymore! I ain't cheering for you lunkheads."

"Most cheerleaders are dancers, Zack – and dancers like doing shows," Candy said calmly. She was still perusing the petition as if she were tempted to sign; twisting her mane so tightly it looked like a long, thick licorice stick. "I don't see why we can't do both."

"Because you can't!"

Zack ripped the petition from her hand and bolted across the room with Darlene in hot pursuit. All eyes followed their wild chase around the cafeteria as a loud crack of thunder rattled the windows. When the lightning follow-up came, they were face-to-face in the aisle next to us, breathing heavily. Nostrils flaring. An irresistible force meeting an immovable object – or however that thing goes. And the lunchroom monitor was nowhere in sight.

"Give it!" Darlene ordered, jutting out her hand.

"Shove it!"

Zack slowly and joyfully proceeded to rip her *Annie* petition into a million pieces while his cohorts cheered him on from their table. Darlene watched as the last piece of paper hit the floor; then she grabbed an unopened bag of potato chips from our table and punch-popped it in Zack's face.

"You die, Deluca!"

Chips shot up into the air and rained down on us like confetti. Cafeteria ladies were scurrying around in the background, like water buffalo fleeing a tsunami. Some kids ran too, but I sat tight and let the chips fall where they may.

"C'mon, you guys," I pleaded. "This isn't how civilized middle-schoolers settle their –"

Before I could finish my sentence, Zack clobbered Darlene with a lime Jell-O surprise and she let out a bloodcurdling scream. Just then lighting flashed across her face. I wish I'd had my camera because I swear she was a dead ringer for the Wicked Witch of the West. Maggie and some other girls came rushing to her defense; and the Fireballs were scrambling over tables to back up Zack.

"Kill the drama geeks!" Tyler hollered, slicing the air with a banana-sword.

Pepper joined the action too, countering with, "Kill the no-neck basketball freaks!"

"Yo!" I cried out. "What're you doin', man?"

"If you can't beat 'em –"

Then the whole cafeteria went ballistic – I'm talking *major* food fight! It was unreal. Sandwich buns spun across the room like helicopter blades. Oranges were catapulted through an onslaught of Twinkie torpedoes and corn kernels. Meatball bombs dropped. Juice-box grenades exploded. The air was thick with the four basic food groups!

Being a pacifist, I ducked under the table for cover. Plus, I didn't want to ruin the only stain-free shirt I owned. A split second later Wally buckled under too.

"Hey, you gonna finish your chocolate milk?" he said, dragging his bassoon down with him. "Grab it for me. It's just gonna go to waste."

"Jeez, what a mooch. We're in the middle of a war here."

"C'mon! I'll thumb wrestle you for it."

"That's your answer to everything."

I peeked over the edge of the table, barely dodging a Grubbs-seeking pickle missile. Just as I reached for the milk carton, a loud whistle blast came from the doorway. It was Coach Mockler.

"Time out! Time out!" he shouted, and blew his whistle so hard that it shot out of his mouth. Everything came to a sudden standstill except for half a PB&J sandwich that was sliding down the wall.

"Holy . . . holy . . . holy," Mockler uttered. He couldn't quite get the "cow" out of his mouth. "In my twelve years at this school I have never seen anything like this! This place is really going to pot. Holy . . . holy . . . holy . . ."

After Mockler's blessing, questions were asked; fingers were pointed; and Darlene and Zack were collared. They were slip-sliding past me en route to Principal Futterman's office when I heard Zack mutter, "You're goin' down, Grubbs."

"Huh?" I was totally confused. "What'd *I* do?"

"Dunno. But wherever you show your ugly face, disaster always follows."

Warped logic. But definitely food for thought.

Chapter 7

Bubbling Trouble

After school I practically froze to death in my flimsy jacket, puddle-hopping over to the Buttermilk Falls Public Library. The endless rain had washed away any traces of summer weather, and the temperature had dropped suddenly, like, don't look now but, *poof*, it's fall. I wanted to beat the rush and get first dibs on all things *Oliver!* at the library – but they ended up only having one CD of the 1963 original Broadway cast recording and a DVD of the 1968 movie. So I checked them both out along with *An Actor Prepares* and a book on foreign dialects, shoved them into my backpack, and splashed my way home. This kid had some prep work to do!

"Dustin? Is that you?" Mom called as I was speed-clomping my way upstairs. "Come down here."

"In a second!"

Even with an umbrella I'd gotten totally drenched. I dropped the good-for-nothing thing on the floor and was peeling off my waterlogged jeans when I realized I was being watched. LMNOP's cat was stretched across my pillow, staring at me in my tighty-whities with her creepy yellow eyes.

"Umm, excuse me, fuzz face," I snapped, grabbing a pair of sweatpants for cover, "but this isn't a free show." I quickly hopped into them and seized the peeping-Tom-cat. She purred at first, then turned and hissed at me when I dropped her onto the floor. "Love me or hate me, tuna breath. Pick one."

A picture postcard was sitting on the hairy pillow where Cinnamon had been. Mom must've brought it up to my room. ANNISQUAN LIGHTHOUSE, the caption read, GLOUCESTER, MASSACHUSETTS. *Jeez, LMNOP wasted no time.* I flipped it over to see what she had to say on the back:

> Hi, Dustin Grubbs,
> We're here and it's so spectacular!
> Guess what?
> I'VE GOT BANGS!!

She still manages to annoy me from clear across the United States. I flung the postcard into the trash can; then emptied out my backpack onto my bed. A piece of paper was stuck to the DVD – the permission slip for our field trip. I sat on the edge of my bed half-reading it, half-yanking off my wet socks. They stretched three times their normal size before finally springing off. I gave them a quick sniff (gross, I know, but it's an automatic thing) and pitched them across the room. Back to the permission slip . . .

```
      to be signed by a parent or guardian granting
      my son/daughter permission to participate in
      the one-day field trip to the Shedd Aquarium
      of Chicago.
```

"Mrrr-oow!" All of a sudden Cinnamon bolted, and my umbrella popped open, showering me with cold rain. An icy shiver shot from my head to my shins.

"Of Chicago?" I blurted out loud. "Hold on a second. That's Dad's home turf!"

A true "watershed" moment, if there ever was one.

How could I have missed the Chicago part when Lynch brought it up on the first day of school? Must've been distracted by Candy's recent developments.

"A free trip to see Dad in the Windy City! No way."

"Dustin!" Mom called again. "Come downstairs!"

I sat there wiping my wet face on my T-shirt, letting the news sink in. I hadn't seen Dad in over *three* years and the thought of coming face-to-face with him made my teeth itch – but in a good way. The more I thought about it, the more excited I got. My heart was rumbling up a storm – I mean it was actually giving the storm outside a run for its money. It's a wonder the thing didn't burst in my chest.

BANG!!

Maybe it just did.

What the heck was that? After I scraped myself off the ceiling I realized the sound had come from downstairs. *Could be Gordy's fireworks accidentally going off in the basement.* But it was just a single blast – like a gunshot. *Is one of the Grubbs packing heat? Man, how much excitement can a kid take in twenty-four hours?*

I darted into the hall and flew down the steps, holding my breath all the way. My family was huddled in the middle of the living room. Aunt Olive was in tears. *Did Granny finally crack and plug the deliveryman from Gleason's Market for busting her eggs again?*

"Dustin, come here," Mom said, gesturing me over.

Was she nuts? I didn't want to see the body up close.

"You and your brother can have ginger ale for the toast."

Ginger ale and toast? I moved in a little closer to the crime scene. Aunt Olive was pouring from a big, green bottle, filling everyone's glasses with bubbles.

"It's a little warm, I'm afraid," Aunt Olive said, sniffling. "The store didn't carry refrigerated champagne."

Oh, I get it. Cork. Pop. Celebration!

"Well, I'll be a monkey's uncle," Granny said, watching

bubbles fill her glass. "Didn't think I'd be alive and kickin' to see another wedding around here."

"Wedding?" I asked, "*Whose* wedding?"

Maybe Gordy's? He'd been dating his girlfriend Rebecca longer than any other girl (and there'd been plenty). But he was barely seventeen. I was pretty sure you weren't allowed to get married until you were eighteen – unless you lived in Vegas or the Ozarks.

"Here's to the blushing bride!" Aunt Birdie said, raising her glass.

"What blushing bride?" I asked, but my words got lost in the clinking of the glasses. *Oh, gawd, it's Mom! Was she dating behind our backs again? And just when things were going so good with Dad.* Panic started to kick in.

"Oooh, that tickles," Aunt Birdie said, giggling into her glass. "The bubbles went straight up my nose."

"Who's getting married?" I asked again, louder this time.

"That would be me!" Aunt Olive said, wiggling her fingers to show off her glittery ring. "I'm officially engaged!"

Instant relief. "Well, congratulations!" I gave my aunt an enthusiastic hug. Maybe *too* enthusiastic – tears came gushing out of her like a fire hydrant.

"Dustin, why don't you help your brother with the hors d'oeuvres?" Mom said, gesturing to the dining room table.

"Ugh. You shouldn't let him near food without rubber gloves and a hairnet."

I had to wrestle the can of cheese away from Gordy before he sprayed it all down his throat. He bolted and I sat there squirting smiley faces on crackers until the platter was filled; then started making rounds like a cater-waiter. Good practice for when I'm a struggling actor in New York, taking odd jobs to make ends meet. I can't wait.

"Oh, none for me, hon," Aunt Olive said, waving me away. "I'm on a strict diet. I've got my eye on a gorgeous wedding dress, and I don't want to look like the great white whale when I march down the aisle."

"White?" Granny spit a mouthful of champagne back into her glass. "That's a cockamamy idea if you ask me. You're not exactly a spring chicken, you know."

"I'm wearing white, Ma. Possibly bone or ecru, but definitely in the white family."

"So, who's the lucky guy?" I asked, changing the subject before there really *was* a dead body lying on the floor.

"You know Smashum Pest Control, right?" Aunt Olive's eyes lit up. "Well, Dennis Smashum is the proprietor, and we've been keeping each other's company for a little over a year now. One thing led to another and – we've set the date! October eighth, so mark your calendars." She did a kind of slow twirl across the floor. "It's always been my dream to get married in a small family ceremony out back – under the rose trellis."

"Oh, *plllllgh*!" Granny made her opinion clear with a sloppy raspberry. "Have you lost your marbles? You'll be freezing your bloomers off."

"Dennis prefers cold weather," my aunt told her, swooning into the cushy, blue armchair. "No bugs."

"Oopsy daisy," Aunt Birdie snorted. "She's lost her ball bearings."

"Just bearings – no ball," I said, correcting her. "Hey, you guys, since the champagne is flowing, I've got some good news too I'd like to –"

"Someone has had enough," Granny interrupted and grabbed the glass from Aunt Olive. The future Mrs. Smashum was obviously too smashed to care.

"So, guess what?" I hopped up on the ottoman to get their attention. "Guys? *Guys!*" All eyes were on me now, but I wasn't sure where to start. I was tempted to just blurt out the Chicago news, but figured I'd better not. Granny always got cranky when anyone mentioned anything to do with Dad. She was still holding a major grudge for him walking out on us like he did. Better to go with my less touchy news.

"I'll be back on the boards again this year! That's theatre-talk for doing a show. We're doing a musical this time – a joint effort between our school and Fenton High. And it's gonna be huge."

"Oh, how wonderful, honey," Mom said over Aunt Birdie's enthusiastic applause. "Which musical are they doing?"

"*Oliver!* You know, based on *Oliver Twist*? I'll be tackling the role of the Artful Dodger. He's a pickpocket – a scallywag, and 'e kinda tawks loik this." I slipped into my cockney accent to really set the mood. "Wears a top hat, 'e does, and works for the oily Mister Fagin – scouring the foggy streets of London to rip off respectable gentlemen and the like."

"Nobody cares," Gordy grumbled.

"It's gonna be a sellout," I said, switching back to my real voice, "just like Gordy. So if anyone wants to give me their ticket orders now and pay in advance, I do accept credit cards –"

"Put me down for two!" Aunt Olive cried out and kicked off her shoes.

"You lie like a rug, dweeb," Gordy snarled. "The sign-up sheets just went up today. You can't know what part you're gonna get if they didn't even hold the stupid auditions yet."

"A mere technicality."

"Aren't you putting the horse before the cart?" Aunt Birdie asked.

"Uh, sorta, but ... wait – it's the *cart* before the horse, isn't it?"

"Don't be silly. How could the cart roll if the horse wasn't pulling it?"

I give up.

Without warning, Gordy shoved me off the ottoman and I hit the carpet like a sack of turtles.

"Hey, I wasn't done!"

"Tough. I've got an announcement to make too." He sat with his ankle crossed over his knee on the edge of the ottoman, waggling his foot a million miles a minute. "You guys might want to sit down for this."

Uh-oh. Mom and Granny took a seat on the couch. I dashed over to the phone and positioned my finger on the nine, just in case I had to dial 911. The Grubbses were famous for their overreactions.

Gordy's face was all twitchy. He probably got caught for drinking beer on school property again, and this time they were throwing him in the slammer for five to ten. No great loss. *Hey, if the wall between our two bedrooms isn't load bearing, we could tear it down and I could have one gigantic –*

"What is it, Gordon?" Mom was using her worried voice.

"All right, I'll just spit it out." But he didn't. "This might freak you out – but I'm not kidding around or anything. This is for real."

Omigod, he's joined a cult!

"I'm – I've decided to go to college."

Dead silence.

"Bartender or clown?" I asked.

"Shaddup, Freakshow!"

"Oh, Gordy!" Mom gushed. "That's incredible news!"

Ten to one it's Rebecca's idea. That girl deserves a medal.

"Well, I can't be too choosy about colleges 'cause of my grades. That's what Becca says." *See!* "Plus, I ain't got no extracurricular activities on my record. But I've still got my senior year to bust my behind, right? And at least I made up my mind to go – if we can afford it."

Mom was beaming. "We'll find a way," she said. "I'm just so proud!"

There was a crack of thunder outside, and I realized Gordy had just stolen mine. I sauntered across the room and perched on the radiator, listening to the outpouring of encouragement raining down on my brother. Here's the thing about juvenile delinquents: Everyone's so used to them being in trouble, just a hint of something respectable eeks out of them and suddenly they're heroes. If you've been on the honor roll your whole life, no one even blinks when you get all A's on your report card again. It's no big whoop. "What's that, Dustin? Oh, you've just won the Pulitzer Prize? That's nice. Now move out of the way of the TV – we can't see through you."

"This house is going to seem so empty next year," Aunt Birdie said dreamily. A series of rapid-fire hiccups escaped, taking her by surprise. "Ooh, pardon me. What with Gordy off at college – *hic* – and Olive moving to Hinkleyville . . ."

"I'm pretty sure I'll end up at the community college," Gordy said between taking hits of air from the empty can-o-cheese. "So I ain't movin' nowhere prob'ly."

"Ain't movin' nowhere prob'ly," I echoed. "Mmm, you keep talking real good English like that and you'll make the dean's list for sure!"

"Bite me, scrod."

"Whoa, back up a minute," Granny said, zeroing in on the bride-to-be. "Let me get this straight. *You're* moving out of the house, Olive? Out of Buttermilk Falls – for good?"

My aunt sat upright. Her eyes were darting around like she was trying to do math in her head. "Of course. What'd you think?"

"I didn't think," Granny snapped. "You didn't give us time to think. You just sprang this whole thing on us at the last minute."

You could feel all the joy in the room fizzling out, like the bubbles in the champagne.

"Dennis's brother has a thriving extermination business in Hinkleyville and – to make a *shong* story *lort,* they've decided to partner up," Aunt Olive said, twisting her engagement ring like she was trying to unscrew her finger. "It makes good business sense. And, besides, it's not that far away."

"Might as well be on the moon." Granny's mouth formed a tight pucker, as if she were fighting to keep the rest of her words locked inside.

"Oh, Ma," Aunt Birdie said, "don't be such a party – *hic* – pooper. She'll come visit us, and we can visit her ... and she'll come visit us ..."

Nobody said anything after that. There was just the *tick-tick-tick* of the wall clock and the *hic-hic-hic* of Aunt Birdie. You could definitely feel the "tension you could cut with a knife" that everyone talks about. Finally, Granny struggled off the couch and shuffled around the room fluffing pillows that didn't need fluffing and straightening pictures that didn't need straightening. My butt was getting deep-fried, so I popped off the radiator and started cleaning up. I swept the crumbs off the dining room table and grabbed the empty champagne bottle.

"A delightfully refreshing nonalcoholic alternative to traditional sparkling wine" was printed in tiny letters on the bottom of the label. *"Contains less than 0.3 % alcohol by volume."* Somehow my aunts had gotten sloshed on sugar water and bubbles. Pretty hysterical, but definitely not a good time to poke fun. I followed Granny into the kitchen, keeping a safe distance, but I could still hear her grumbling to herself:

"First Teddy – now Olive. Running off with some bug man – to Hinkleyville, of all places. Might as well be on the doggone moon."

Chapter 8

Three Lawyers, an Aardvark, and a Substitute Teacher . . .

"Thanks, Ted. I haven't laughed that hard in quite a while. It's been kind of intense around here lately – I really needed that!" Mom was winding up her phone conversation with Dad, wiping her eyes from busting a gut. After being incommunicado for a third of a decade due to Mom's righteous anger, my crazy parents were hitting it off these days better than ever. Now he was causing happy tears – not sad. A complete 180.

"Okay, I'll hand you over to your son now. Yeah, talk to you soon, hon."

Hon? Move over Aunt Olive – was there another wedding in the works? I took the phone and heard Dad's voice radiating through.

"Hey, kid! So, break a leg at that audition of yours. When is it again?"

"Tomorrow after school. I'm singing your favorite song – the 'Broadway' one. And Aunt Olive helped me with it, so I'm not too worried. She said it doesn't matter too much if I can hit all the high notes, the important thing is that I sell it."

"And if you screw up, just launch into a joke or something. Funny never fails."

"Right."

"Play up your strengths and they won't notice your weaknesses."

"Got it."

"Wow 'em with a big finish and they'll forgive you for anything."

"Hey, read my lips. I said I wasn't worried."

"I can't read your lips – we're on the phone."

"Good one. You should be a comedian."

"Haaa! Let's see . . . what else can I tell ya?"

"There's that thing about picturing everyone in their underwear, but that's just wrong."

"Oh, wait – I know. I was gonna say drink a lot of water. It'll keep your phlegm down and your energy up."

"Copy, good buddy."

"I've got a few surprises up my sleeve for when we meet in Chicago, so stand warned. On the twenty-third, right?"

"Right. See you then."

"Okeydokey, smokey."

"Later, dude – I mean Dad!"

*　　*　　*

The next day after the three-fifteen bell, all auditioners were told to congregate in the cafeteria, which was being used as a kind of holding tank. Bad idea. Ever since the janitors cleaned up after the food war, it smelled like a combination of fish sticks and industrial-strength pine. *Eesh!* I was queasy enough already with my first big musical audition just minutes away – I didn't want a repeat of that dance studio incident.

"Okay, kiddles," Miss Van Rye said, poking her head into the cafeteria, "we'll be starting in just a few minutes and you'll be going into the auditorium in groups of ten. So when I call your name, form a line at the door. Quick like bunnies!"

Dad's advice about drinking a lot of water seemed to be panning out – I had energy to spare and no sign of phlegm. Miss Van Rye was leading my group to the backstage area and I topped off my tank with a few final sips from the water fountain. When I looked up at the bulletin board where the sign-up sheet had hung, there was a DANCE IS MY SPORT! bumper sticker plastered over the one that said SPORTS RULE!

"If you have sheet music, hand it to the accompanist, then stand center stage and announce your song," Miss Van Rye said in a hushed voice while we formed a tight, sweaty line in the stage-right wings. "And for goodness sake, only one song per customer unless they specifically ask to hear more. Break legs, munchkins!"

I was fifth in line behind Stewy Ziggler. It kind of surprised me that he showed up, but I was sure glad he did – he being a boy and all. Plus, it was good to see that mini-egghead coming out of his shell. He looked as if he were waiting in line for the guillotine, though, and I think he was releasing toxic nerve gas.

"C'mon, give us a break," I said, fanning the air. "Are you cutting SBDs?"

"Huh?" he asked.

"Silent-but-deadlies?"

Stewy sniffed the air all around him, looking like one of those bobble-head dolls. "Not that I'm aware."

I was expecting maybe a "he who smelt it dealt it." Why was he talking like some snooty butler?

"You're not fooling anyone. Just try clenching, will ya? I'm suffocating here."

Darlene's name was called first, and she ripped off her sweater to reveal a bright red Orphan Annie dress, spouting, "Watch and learn!" I'll be darned if she didn't spin out onstage and sing a medley of practically the entire score from *Annie*. *Jeez, what a hardhead! The Arts Committee had already turned down her stupid petition and announced we were definitely doing* Oliver! *Talk about pushy.* She finished by belting out the song "Tomorrow" and sliding into the splits; then she asked the casting people if they wanted to hear a ballad that showed off her soprano range. It sounded like a unanimous "no," but Darlene, being Darlene, launched right into, "The hills are alive with the sound of –"

"You suck!"

Someone had shouted it from the back of the house.

Man, I thought, *tough crowd.*

Darlene stopped singing. There was a door slam; a loud commotion. Silence.

"What's going on out there?" Stewy asked me, all wide-eyed and fidgety. "What's happening?"

"Got me."

I peeked around the black curtains with the other auditioners trying to see what the deal was in the auditorium. Finally Darlene stomped passed us, complaining, "Some juvenile delinquent's out there yelling stuff! Gawd, this is so unprofessional."

Hopefully the heckler wouldn't be back during my five-minute time slot!

"You did awesome, Dar," Maggie gushed as Miss Van Rye rushed her out onto the stage next. When I heard her lyrics about "washing that man right outta my hair" being sung over and over, I got a sudden urge to go to the bathroom. Sudden and severe. I motioned to Miss Van Rye, who came trotting over. She seemed on edge.

"May I take a time-out for a potty break? It's just number one. I'll be quick as a bunny." You have to appeal to kindergarten teachers on their level.

"Oh, hon, you're up after Stewart. With that disruption we've lost precious time, and I just want to keep things flowing."

Flowing – yeow!

"Is it an emergency or do you think you can brave it out?" she asked, her eyes penetrating mine. "The drama teachers from Fenton High are out there and I don't want to make waves."

Waves – eesh!

"I can suck it up, I guess."

"That's my little trouper."

I was going over my song lyrics in my head to get my mind off all things H$_2$O. Stewy was up next. Someone from the back of the line yelled, "Good luck, squirt." *Squirt – ooh!* But when he opened his mouth to sing, he was interrupted by more distant taunts and door slamming.

"Geeks!" "Nerds!" "Losers!" "Turds!"

"If I catch you boys, I'll see to it that you're suspended for life!" Futterman bellowed from somewhere in the auditorium.

From the wings poor Stewy looked so worked up I thought they were going to have to call in the paramedics. He attempted his song a second and third time, but kept screwing up the lyrics. In the meantime, my teeth were floating, like Granny says, and I had to bounce up and down to keep my sprinkler system from going off.

"Stewart, sweetie, just relax," Miss Honeywell said from the center of the house in her soothing Southern twang. "You're getting all flustered, bless your heart. Principal Futterman's taking care of things right now, so we won't have any more rude interruptions."

"Uh, maybe this was a mistake," Stewy said, inching toward the wings.

"No, you're doing great, pum'kin. Maybe try singing something you're more familiar with, like – oh, I don't know – 'Happy Birthday' or 'Row, Row, Row Your Boat.'"

No boats!

I tried to stick it out, but when he got to "gently down the stream," I had to haul butt swiftly down the hall – to the john. My bladder was about to splatter! *Thanks for the great advice, Pop.* My heart was thumping like a bass drum as I push-push-pushed to answer nature's call.

On my way out of the bathroom I caught a glimpse of Zack, Tyler, and Pig tearing up the back steps. Talk about a triple threat! They were obviously the meatheads yelling stuff, which came as no surprise. But I wasn't going to rat on them, because Zack already hated my guts and I didn't want the whole basketball team out to get me.

"Dustin Grubbs! Where did he disappear to?" I heard Miss Van Rye call as I flew toward backstage. "There go my ulcers. Last call for Dustin Gru –"

"I'm here!"

I took a deep breath and let the tension blow out of me. Waterlogged no more, I walked onto that stage as if I owned it. Relaxed. Confident. Dare I say dazzling? I felt bad for Stewy, but after his train wreck of an audition I was going to knock 'em dead – hecklers or not.

The pianist turned out to be Mrs. Sternhagen, my old second-grade teacher. I don't know why I was so surprised. She played "The Star Spangled Banner" at every assembly and was pretty good at tickling the ivories. Still, I had her pegged as an enemy of the arts. She greeted me with her usual glacial stare.

"Did you bring sheet music?"

"Uh – no, was I supposed to?" I didn't wait for an answer. "I'm singing 'Give My Regards to Broadway.' You know that one, right? It's my dad's favorite."

She thumbed through a big, thick book of songs that was sitting on the piano, clicking her tongue.

"Here it is. You're very lucky," she said, pushing her glasses up her pointed nose. "Are you taking it from the verse or the chorus?"

What's the difference?

"Take it from the top," I said, as if I knew what I was talking about.

I strutted to center stage, where the stage lights were hotter than I'd remembered. Mrs. Sternhagen's rancid perfume must've followed me. It smelled like Stewy Ziggler in a petunia patch.

"Dustin Grubbs," I announced to the faceless blobs sitting in the dark auditorium. "'Give My Regards to Broadway.' Hit it!"

"What tempo?" Sternhagen asked.

Man, I didn't know there was gonna be a pop quiz.

"Uh, medium, please." I was just guessing, but that was the way I ordered my burgers and it always worked out pretty well.

She played a fancy introduction, but I wasn't sure exactly when to jump in. I must've gotten distracted by Futterman pacing the rear of the auditorium, policing the joint. Sternhagen stopped and gave me a sharp look, then played the intro again.

"No, no. 'Give My Regards,'" I told her, "'to Broadway.' That's not it."

"That's the verse. You said to take it from the top, didn't you?"

"Yes, ma'am, but I think I meant a different top."

"Why don't you just take it from the refrain?"

"Okay." *Whatever that is. Just get on with it – this is embarrassing.*

Mrs. Sternhagen played a shorter intro this time and hit one key on the piano to give me my starting note. I hummed it to myself, but my brain couldn't match it.

What the heck's happening to me? Finding the starting note is the easiest part!

"Give . . ." I sang. But that wasn't it. She hit the piano key again. "Give – give – give – " And again, and again. Her arm flab was jiggling as she pounded that one key a thousand times, but I could *not* for the life of me find my starting note.

"Mr. Grubbs, you're simply not hearing it," Mrs. Sternhagen complained, followed by an annoyed, drawn-out sigh. I could tell that her patience, like the underarms of her drab, brown dress, was wearing thin. Then she went and did it. She turned to the auditioners in the audience and uttered the two deadliest words in the world of musical theatre: "Pitch problems."

"Only in baseball!" I blurted out, coming to my own defense. "It might be my earwax buildup – that runs in our family."

"Well, be that as it may," the Devil Woman said, banging the life out of that one yellow piano key, "you still should be able to reproduce the correct note instantaneously, unless –" A look of horror washed over her face. "You're not *tone-deaf*, are you?" She said it in an anxious half-voice, like when my aunts whisper about feminine products.

"Not that I'm aware."

I could hear the words *tone-deaf* being murmured by the teachers who were deciding my fate. "Tone-deaf!" ringing in the balcony. "Tone-deaf!" echoing off the walls.

"Come stand by the piano." Mrs. Sternhagen waved me over. "Try singing it along with me."

This can't be happening. I felt like one of her slow second-graders.

She plunked out the melody and croaked, "Give my regards to Broadway . . ." I joined in, sounding a little shaky. "Remember me to Herald Square –" My voice cracked. Puberty kicking in, but they'd probably take that into consideration. "Tell all the gang at Forty-second Street that I will soon be there." I was back on track. "Whisper of how I'm yearning . . ." Sternhagen cut out and it was all me, belting it out. "To mingle with the old time throng . . ." Back to full tempo, really working the stage. "Yeah, give my regards to old Broadway" – *wow 'em with a big finish and they'll forgive you for anything* – "and say that I'll – be – there – hair – *looong!*"

I fell to one knee, holding that last note for days. "The money note" Aunt Olive called it, and I milked it for every penny it was worth. When my breath finally ran out I scrambled to my feet and took a quick bow.

Dead silence.

"It's ere long, Mr. Grubbs, not *hair* long," Mrs. Sternhagen finally said, sounding unimpressed. "It means *before* long."

"My mistake."

"Well, at least you got through it."

I stood there smiling into the dark auditorium, waiting for positive feedback – or *any* feedback.

"Thank you, Dustin, very much," Miss Honeywell said in a cheery voice. "Everyone who auditions will be cast in one capacity or another. So if you don't hear from us it simply means we don't need to have you read from the script. Okay, sugar?"

"Okay." *Sugar.*

"Uh, just FYI, I'm getting over a little cold," I lied, "so my throat's still a little scratchy. "And I never heard the piano part before. I could sing something else if you like." *Oh, gawd, I was turning into Darlene.*

"That's all we need for today," Miss Honeywell told me. "That was very nice."

Very nice? Translation: You stunk up the place.

Mrs. Sternhagen hung her head when I passed her on my mile-long trek to the wings. I must've bombed big-time. Just as tears were stinging my eyes, more of Dad's advice flashed in my head: *Play up your strengths and they won't notice your weaknesses. Funny never fails!*

"Wait!" I did an about-face and steamrolled my way to center stage.

"Yes, Mr. Grubbs? What now?"

I recognized that voice – *it's Mr. Lynch! Don't let it throw you.*

"Well . . . ?" he grumbled.

"Okay, three lawyers, an aardvark, and a substitute teacher walk into a bar –"

That's when a bright orange basketball came sailing out of the balcony and hit me right between the eyes.

Chapter 9

SLUDGE

I was too wound up Thursday night to get any shut-eye. My audition disaster was on constant replay in my head – every time I closed my eyes I saw that basketball coming at me. And that "tone-deaf" comment really stuck in my craw – whatever that is. *In a matter of weeks I'd plummeted from a triple threat to a double – to hardly a threat at all!* I'd finally started drifting off, when my mind jumped to the field trip the next day. The plan was to hook up with Dad on Friday after the Shedd Aquarium visit, and spend the whole weekend with him. Just the two of us – well, and the entire city of Chicago. That required mega sleep, but I was vibrating with excitement.

So I clamped my eyes shut and refused to think a single thought about A, the audition; B, the field trip; or C, Dad. But somehow I got to thinking about D, what superpowers I'd want most. *Okay, stop! This is stupid.* I squinted at the 3:04

AM blazing on my digital clock. *If I fall asleep right this second I could still get four and a half good hours. Ready, set, sleep.* Unfortunately, I was still deciding between X-ray vision and the ability to fly when the sun came up.

The bowl of lukewarm oatmeal I wolfed down for breakfast reminded me of the workhouse gruel the orphans in *Oliver!* ate – setting off stomach pangs. But staring at the two pitiful raisins at the bottom of the bowl, I decided I wasn't going to give up hope about being in the musical. *Movie stars are always telling stories about how they loused up their audition but still got the part!* Plus, everybody knows I can act. And I totally saved last year's show – the school owed me. (Not to mention, they really needed boys.)

Okay, maybe I was just kidding myself, but I needed a positive attitude to get through the weekend. So with renewed confidence (sorta) I held out my empty bowl to Mom and uttered Oliver's famous line:

"Please, sir, I want some more."

"I'm late for work. Grab a granola bar if you're still hungry."

We both rushed around the house collecting our things and met up at the kitchen door, where she handed me a sealed envelope. "This has emergency money and phone numbers in it. So don't lose it, whatever you do."

"Mom, have you seen my book, *An Actor Prepares*?" I was rummaging through my overloaded backpack. "I need tons to read for that two-hour bus ride."

"I think I saw it in your brother's room yesterday when I was changing his sheets."

Cripes! He probably scribbled on all the pages so the library will sue me. But I didn't have time to deal with Gord-zilla.

"Listen, Dustin, if you want to cut your visit with your father short – for any reason, just call," Mom reminded me for the thousandth time. "Or if you just feel like talking. Or if you're going to be late meeting me at the Greyhound bus station on Sunday . . . or get sick . . . or just feel like talking . . ."

"You covered that one twice. Don't be doing your mom thing and calling every two seconds checking up on me, okay? Promise?"

"I promise." She stuffed a tissue packet and a small bottle of hand sanitizer into my jacket pockets. "But don't hold me to it. I am your mother after all." There was a long, desperate hug. I felt as if she were sending me off to war.

When I got to school I made a quick bathroom pit stop to make sure I was drained of all liquids before the long trip. It took me a second to realize I was staring at a missing-dog flier that was posted over the urinal. It was Futterman's weird dog, Shatzi. *Hmm. Must've gotten fed up and flown the coop.* Someone had drawn a moustache and an eye patch on the pooch's picture with black marker. Kids can be so cruel.

By the time I got to the buses they were already packed, and some kid in a humongous GOT MUSIC? sweatshirt was sitting next to my best friend.

"Jeez, Wal, thanks for saving me a seat!" I said sarcastically.

"First come, first serve. You snooze, you lose. The early bird gets –"

"The worm. I know. Man, you've been hanging around my family too long, with their crazy sayings." I glared at the giant lump taking up *my* seat with a hard, threatening look. "You're an eighth-grader, right?"

And then it spoke. "Lester Moore."

"Aren't you supposed to be on the other bus?"

"It was too crowded. I got special permission from Miss Sedgwick to ride on this bus, if you must know."

"Take a chill pill. I just asked."

"Get this," Wally said. "Les has been going to our school for two years, but we never met till last summer in band camp." *Band camp, ugh!* "He's an awesome French horn player and he might join my quintet. I'm thinking of calling it Opus Five."

"Fascinating." I waited for more to come out of my mouth but nothing did, so I continued down the aisle.

Les Moore. His name was an oxymoron – more or less. According to Mr. Lynch, that's when contradictory words are combined, like deafening silence or jumbo shrimp. Not sure if it really applied in this case, but from what I could tell, Les Moore was big as an ox and definitely a moron.

"Hey, Dustin!" Stewy called out, waving me down from the backseat of the bus. "There's room back here."

"Hi, Stew, what's new?"

There was always plenty of room around Stewy. Probably because he was too smart, too young, and due to the macrobiotic lunches his Mom packed him – too stinky. Luckily, Pepper and her dad (biological, not step) were stuck in the backseat too. He must've been chaperoning.

"Dust-buster! Long time no see," Mr. Pew said really enthused. "We've got a seat all warmed up for ya." I squeezed in between Pepper and the fingerprint-covered window. "Say, ya ever had a hankering for some really good tomatoes?"

Huh? Mostly after they turn into ketchup or spaghetti sauce, but, "Sure," I replied. "Who hasn't?"

"Wrong answer," Pepper whispered, elbowing me. "Now you'll never shut him up."

"I've got you pegged as a beefsteak tomato type of guy, am I right? I'm partial to those babies myself, but there's quite a variety out there! You've got your Quick Picks, your Supersonics, your Mountain Springs – your orange, your pink, your white . . ."

I laughed out loud just so Wally would think I was having a good time. The bus peeled out of the lot and I took out my foreign-dialects book from my backpack as if to say thanks for sharing, Mr. P., but conversation over. That didn't stop him from rattling on nonstop. I was able to tune him out, though, quietly practicing my cockney accent – hopefully for the show. *Think positive!*

By the time we hit Willowbridge, my tongue needed a break. (You try getting "Bob's your uncle" to sound like "bAWbz y' rAHnkOOl," like, fifty times straight.) So I gazed out the window at the gigantic, head-shape water tower and for some reason pictured Dad's face on it – like that cutout in the attic, only a zillion times bigger. The thought of being up close and personal again with the real thing was freaking me out and I didn't know why. Sure, I hadn't set eyes on him in three years, but we talked all the time. And it's not as if we were strangers – same flesh and blood – plus, he was the funniest father on the planet. But part of me wanted to call the whole thing off. *Just quit while he's a head.*

"Jeez, Pepper, can I have a little breathing room here?" I was jammed up against the window. "You're squashing me like a – tomato."

"I'm just trying to avoid Stewy's stench," she murmured, practically snuggling. "His mom must've packed him those sardine-barley nut balls again."

Enough said. For the rest of the trip I pretended to be asleep, while Mr. Pew jawed on about the horrors of horn-worms and stinkbugs. Finally, I heard the bus engine wheezing to a stop and my eyes popped open. The view from the Shedd Aquarium parking lot alone was totally worth the trip! There was the Chicago skyline on one side with skyscraper after skyscraper poking through wispy clouds; and Lake

Michigan on the opposite side – an ocean of a lake, with no end to its shimmery blue water in sight.

"People, people! Back in your seats!" Mr. Lynch shouted over the bus blabber, waving his spindly, windshield-wiper arms. "The buses will be locked, so please remember to take your lunches, notebooks, asthma inhalers.... Oh, and chaperones, we're two teachers short, so you really need to be on your toes. Principal Futterman was supposed to be accompanying us, but he had a pet emergency; and Coach Mockler pulled a fast one on us at the last minute and decided to 'call in sick.'" He did the air-quote finger gesture like he thought it was a crock. "Okay, everyone, grab your belongings and let's move!"

The aquarium was bigger than Buckingham Palace. (Not that I'd ever measured.) Mr. Lynch told us to take detailed notes because we'd be writing a report on our favorite exhibit. *So many fish, so little time!* Well, fish, mammals, coral, you name it. I'd gotten totally sucked up into water world, but never stopped thinking about the big finale of the day – Dad! I was jotting down report possibilities in my spiral notebook as we moved from exhibit to exhibit. By late afternoon I had it narrowed down to:

1. <u>Beluga Whales</u>. Love to have their tongues tickled! (I'll take the staff's word for that.)

2. <u>Potbelly Seahorses</u>. Males give birth to the babies. (Totally glad I'm not a seahorse.)
3. <u>Poisonous Frogs</u>. The prettier, the deadlier. (Something about that combo that's hard to resist.)

When we stumbled upon the penguin exhibit I melted – on the inside. The outside was pretty chilly. But those birds were so darn cute. I scored the last seat on a long, carpeted bench facing the exhibit, which was packed with noisy little kids in red crab-pincher caps. The penguins were behind a wall of thick glass. Some swimming; some waddling around on a cascading rock wall that was dripping in icicles.

"Hey, Dust," Wally said, running up to me, "you like seafood?"

Even the first-grader sitting next to me rolled his eyes. But you had to indulge the Walrus every now and then.

"Yeah. Why?"

"See – food!" He opened his mouth wide, revealing a chocolatey lump.

"That joke is older than the hills – with dinosaur poop sprinkled on top."

Wally stopped chewing and made a sour face.

"So is this Snickers Bar."

We majorly cracked up, just like old times. But then

the Oxymoron bounded out of nowhere and dragged him away.

"Why's Wally always hanging out with that guy now?" Stewy asked, squeezing in next to me. (And I'd assumed the weird smell was coming from the fish.) "I thought *you* were his best friend."

"I am!"

Wally's booming laughter came from the Oceanarium behind us. The Oxymoron probably told him a joke about Mozart or Schmozart or something.

"Well, don't look now," Stewy said, looking over his shoulder, "but you might have some competition."

"I think that's apparent."

"Nuh-uh, that's an eighth-grader. Lester something. He's just overgrown for his age."

"No, not a *parent* – I meant – oh, skip it."

The crab-cap crew was leaving and a bunch of rowdy boys around my age immediately took their place on the bench. I honed in on the staff guy, who was giving his spiel in front of the exhibit. "We humans can learn a valuable lesson from these feathered creatures . . ." He looked an awful lot like a giant penguin himself. "Most penguins mate for life."

Interesting! I added 4. Penguins after Poisonous Frogs in my notebook and jotted down that little fact. When I looked up I saw Zack and some of the other Fireballs roughhousing down the steps – they ended up standing right in front of us, blocking our view. *Rude with a capital* R. Mr. Kincaid was with them. He'd probably volunteered to chaperone so he could make Zack drop and give him twenty between exhibits.

"Hey, Butterballs! Down in front!" the kid next to me hollered.

"Don't look now," I heard Pig say to Zack, "but the Claymore Cougars are here." Suddenly the human wildlife was more interesting than the penguins. It was almost like the Jets meeting the Sharks in *West Side Story,* only without the switchblades and finger snaps. Their conversation went something like this:

FIREBALLS: Well, if it isn't the Claymore Boogers. We're looking forward to beatin' the snot outta you at the Slam-Dunk Tourney this year.

COUGARS: In your dreams. We whooped your [BLEEP] last year, Butterballs. What makes you think we can't do it again?

FIREBALLS: Duh. Home-court advantage. This year the tourney's on our turf!

COUGARS: [CRACKING UP BIG-TIME] I guess you guys didn't hear. News flash: They're holding the basketball tournament at Claymore again this year!

FIREBALLS: That's bull!

COUGARS: 'Fraid not, Butterballs. The organizers think the athletic facilities at your school belong in the freakin' Stone Age.

FIREBALLS: Liars!

COUGARS: Losers!

Mr. Kincaid and the Fireballs were sizzling mad. Mad enough for a backstreet "rumble." I shot out of my seat and purposely got swallowed up in a clump of plaid-clad Catholic schoolgirls inching toward the penguin display – but I could still hear what Mr. Kincaid was saying. Heck, they could hear it in Bangladesh.

"This is the last straw!" he ranted. "We were looking forward to hosting that tournament for the last four years, and now it's ripped out from under us. Things have really gotten out of hand at that school of yours – pouring all its money into that sissy little play. What's next? Turning the basketball team into a sewing circle? We have *got* to put our foot down before sports don't exist at all in our town!"

I'd ended up at the exhibit railing right next to Candy Garboni, who was wearing a fluorescent orange fur jacket that looked like a limp Muppet. "Whoa," I said, "did you catch that? Mr. Kincaid is really steamed about our musical." She seemed oblivious. "Hey, did you ever end up auditioning? I didn't see you there."

"Nah, I decided to go out for cheerleader instead."

She was cracking her gum, squinting at a pair of penguins zooming through the water like mini-torpedoes. "Look at 'em go!" I said, touching the glass.

"To me they just look like little blur waiters. I can't see so good without my glasses."

"Did you forget 'em?"

"No. But they make me look hideous."

"You can spot several of the birds on their nests at the far right," the penguin guy said, continuing his commentary. "The eggs they're sitting on are actually plastic decoys. We had to transfer the real ones to an incubator, because they'd never hatch in this environment."

"That's not fair, fakin' 'em out like that," I grumbled to Darlene. "Those poor penguins are pouring all their energy into something that's never gonna happen."

"Well, it *is* gonna happen. Just not the way they think."

Wicked laughter erupted from across the aquarium. I craned my neck to see past the blubber-fur-and-feathers display and saw three buzz-cut boneheads bobbing over the edge of the Oceanarium. Who else but Zack, Pig, and Tyler? And it looked like they were taunting the dolphins! Mr. Kincaid was standing there too, not doing a darn thing about it.

"Can you believe those guys?" I could feel the outrage smoldering in my cheeks as I checked out the scene. "Gawd, all those Fireballs are such – such – sludge! Okay, not *all* of them, but Zack and some of those other jocks are just –"

Darlene burst a bubble in my face, following it up with, "Sludge?"

"S-L-U-D-G-E. Slimy, slobbery, muck-sucking, low-life sludge." *Why is there never a teacher around when you need one? Or a chaperone?* "Look, now they're actually throwing stuff in the water! That better not be pennies!" With no time to waste, I fumed up the steps toward the crime scene, practically ramming into good-for-nothing Mr. Kincaid.

"Knock it off, you guys! Can't you read the signs? 'Coins can kill! If swallowed, they can lodge in an animal's stomach, causing ulcers, infections, and even *death.*'"

"Up yours, tool!" "Get bent!" "Beat it, drama queen!"

Just in the nick, a security guard flew onto the scene and marshaled the culprits away from the Oceanarium and into the tented-in area at the registered group entrance. "The boys were just having a little fun," Mr. Kincaid called out, running after them. *Jerk!* I was left alone – shaken. Staring at a clinging sea star.

Everything seemed to be under control again until I gazed down at my watch. 4:58! If I were a whale, a spray of adrenaline would've shot out my blowhole. *Dad's supposed to meet me by the man-holding-the-giant-fish fountain outside, like – now!*

My heart was sputtering as I sprinted out to the fountain next to the parking lot. I had my eyes peeled for a black sedan because Dad said he'd be picking me up in a limo. *Okay, get a grip,* I told myself. It wasn't too long before my classmates were piling onto the buses in the distance, and I starting thinking "what if he doesn't show up?" thoughts. I'd be stranded. I mean, look at his track record. *What if he pulls another Dad stunt?*

Just as both Buttermilk Falls buses were pulling out of the

lot, some maniac cab came tearing past them, zigzagging through Section DD-HH. It zoomed past me and the driver shouted, "Welcome to the windy city!" through a bullhorn. The license plate number was a blur. But the cab had a blue sign lit up on the roof that read: LuvQUEST.com and something about "finding your soul mate in the urban jungle." I jotted that down in my notebook in case I had to report this wack-job.

When I looked up, there it was – Dad's black limo! Just pulling into the parking lot. That psycho taxicab almost crashed right into it!

"...Home of Wrigley Field," the cabbie shouted, sticking his head out his window. He was done up in clown makeup with a rainbow Afro wig. *Gawd, what a freak.* "...the Bears, the Magnificent Mile – umm, deep-dish pizza. Welcome to Chi-town, Dustin Grubbs!"

The taxicab came to a screeching stop right in front of me. My jaw just about hit the pavement along with my spiral notebook.

"What's the matter, kid, don't you recognize your ol' man?"

Chapter 10

Where the Rubber Nose Hits the Road

"Get in, get in!" blasted through the bullhorn. I went for the back door of the cab. "No, no, you're riding shotgun. Sit up front with me!"

As soon as we pulled away, a wave of fear splashed through me. Big, spooky city – big, nutcase clown – what was I getting myself into? I untwisted my seat belt and fastened the cold buckle with a sharp and final *click*.

"It's great to see you, Dusty! I really missed you, kid!" He leaned over and grazed my forehead with a scratchy kiss. It sounded like Dad, but I still wasn't 100 percent sure if he was really my father or Zippo the Kidnapping Clown. *Would it be rude to ask to see three forms of ID?*

"It's great to see you too – I think."

"Ouch! Way to hurt your ol' man right outta the gate."

"Oh, no, I didn't mean it like that, Dad." *If that is your real name.* "It's just – you said you were picking me up in a limo. And what's with the clown thing?"

"This *is* my limo – and I know how much you've always loved clowns."

"Dad, I hate clowns. Gordy loves clowns."

I felt my toes clench. We were definitely off to a rocky start.

"Oh – well, I guess I screwed that up." Dad pinched off his red rubber nose and tossed it out the window. Someone honked a horn. "There. All better?"

He still had a giant red mouth painted on, though – not to mention blue eyebrows and a ruffle collar.

"So, since when do you drive a cab?"

"Since my landlord insisted on being paid in money instead of knock-knock jokes." He laughed. I didn't. "Man, oh, man, go ahead and check out my hack license if you want. I won't be insulted. It's right there in front of you."

There was a blurry head shot on his ID card hanging on the dashboard. It could've been the Easter Bunny, for all I knew. Okay, it had "Theodore Grubbs" plastered across the top of it, but for some reason I still had my doubts. But when we turned onto Lake Shore Drive, he ripped off his curly wig and tossed it onto the backseat and I knew it was Dad for sure. His receding hairline had moved farther north, but the familiar 3-D mole constellation on his temple was definite proof. He'd always told us that if you connected the dots it'd form –

"The Big Dipper!" I exclaimed with a sense of relief.

The wig had left a purplish imprint across his forehead – it looked as if you could screw the top of his head off and paper snakes would jump out. Just as I was starting to breathe easy, I wasn't sure I wanted to breathe at all.

"No offense, Pop, but what reeks?"

The little cardboard pine tree deodorizer dangling off the rearview mirror must've expired because the cab smelled like an armpit bouquet.

"*Err,* it could be the Italian beef sandwich I brought you. They don't make 'em like this anywhere else but Chicago. It's delish. Go ahead, dig in."

I debagged half the sandwich and took a cautious, drippy bite. "Hah and oosey!" I said with a mouthful.

"Huh? Oh, hot and juicy," he echoed, handing me a cold, wet can of Mountain Dew. "So, did you have a *whale* of a good time at the aquarium? Are you an expert on coral reefs and mollusks now?"

"Nuh-uh." I swallowed fast and popped open the can of soda. "But if you're interested in the history of the tomato, I'm your man."

"How's that?"

"Pepper's dad chaperoned, and he couldn't stop blabbering about his tomato patch – and his strawberry patch –"

"All I've got is a nicotine patch. Bah-*dum*-pum!"

He usually "bah-*dum*-pummed" after cracking a joke. Like back in the vaudeville days when the drummer would play a rim shot after a comic delivered his punch line. Corny, but effective.

"Nicotine patch," he repeated, getting a bigger kick out of it than the first time. "I should write that one down. Maybe I can work it into my act." He peeled a long, curly blue hair off his cheek and flicked it away. "Say, how'd that audition of yours pan out? You were so worked up about it – did you knock 'em dead?"

"Something like that."

All of a sudden a speeding minivan cut in front of us and Dad grabbed his bullhorn and yelled "Maniac!" out the window. "Where'd that guy learn to drive?" he asked me. "Sears Roebuck? Bah-*dum* –"

"Actually, Dad," I interrupted, "Sears *does* have a driving school."

That ended up being a real conversation killer, which was just as well – I didn't feel like spilling my guts about my audition disaster anyway. Still, I should've let him get out his final "pum." With my sandwich in one hand and my soda in the other, I sunk deep into the ripped vinyl, taking in the incredible view. Downtown Chicago on the left side looked as if it were decorated in an endless strand of twinkle lights – and Lake Michigan, to my right, turned a glittery purple and eventually disappeared, blending seamlessly with the night sky. The taxi made a jerky left turn off Lake Shore Drive and Dad leaned over and tore a bite out of my sandwich, growling like a lion with fresh kill in his teeth. He was obviously begging for a reaction.

"Hey, Dad, you like seafood?" I said out of desperation.

"Who doesn't?"

We turned to each other with mouths wide open. "See – *food*!" We spouted at the same time. "Bah-*dum*-pum!"

It was perfect timing. We really yucked it up. Who knew that Wally's lame kindergarten joke would put us right back on track?

"So," Dad said, sucking in a dangling green pepper, "on a scale from one to ten, how badly does your grandmother hate my guts?"

"She doesn't hate you."

If I were Pinocchio, my nose would be poking through the windshield.

"Don't kid a kidder, kid."

"Okay, about a fifty-seven, but you didn't hear it from me."

We must've drove around for hours while Dad talked my ear off, asking questions about the family and pointing out the sights. The Sears Tower, one of the tallest buildings in the world; Navy Pier with its giant Ferris wheel; the water tower where Mrs. O'Leary's cow knocked over a lantern and started the Great Chicago Fire.

"What about your mom – is she seeing anyone?"

Mountain Dew shot out of my mouth. I hadn't seen that one coming! But I have to admit, it was exactly the kind of question I was hoping for.

"She sees lots of people." I was playing it ultracool.

"You know what I mean. Somebody special?"

"A foot specialist – for her bunions."

"Wisenheimer."

Mom had sworn me to secrecy about her love life, but here's the real scoop: She had dated her boss at the Donut Hole, but that went stale quicker than their day-old crullers. Then there was Dr. Devon, who was "perfect on paper" but there wasn't any "chemistry" so she broke things off "before anyone got hurt." I think she went and got hurt anyway, and quit trying altogether after that.

"You wouldn't be holdin' out on your ol' man now, would ya? Don't be afraid to come right out with it – you won't hurt my feelings."

"Cripes," I mumbled, sopping up soda under my rear end with the napkins. "This is turning into a sticky situation."

"I knew it." He ripped off his ruffle collar, looking disturbed.

"Huh? No, not Mom – the Mountain Dew! Jeez, if you gotta know, sure, she's dated around a little – especially since she found your old weights in the attic and started working out. She's turning into one of those mom-babes." I figured a little carrot-dangling couldn't hurt. "But why the tenth degree? You talk to her all the time on the phone."

"She doesn't tell me everything, Dusty."

"Me either."

"Well," Dad said, pondering it over, "you know your ma – both she and God work in mysterious ways."

So does her son. Suddenly he slammed on the brakes, and we went lunging forward – then back – then forward. "We're here!" he announced, turning off the ignition. The cab was parked halfway on the curb. "That'll be seventy-three fifty. Plus tip."

"You live *here*?"

"Just three nights a week."

I thought Dad was exaggerating when he called the comedy club where he performed "a hole in the wall," but it turns out he was right. Anyone would walk right past the Laugheteria if it weren't for the nonstop laugh track they had blasting out front. I wondered how the bum we had to step over in the doorway was sleeping so soundly. There was a sleazy uneasiness that hit me when we walked into the place, yet I couldn't wait to check it out.

"Hey, Morty, I know this is kinda last minute but can you put me in the lineup for tonight?" Dad asked a short, bald guy wiping down the bar. I could barely even see his face through the curtain of smoke pouring from his cigar.

"Yeah, I can probably squeeze ya in," Morty growled, scratching his potbelly. "But some talent scout's supposed to be in the audience for the first show, so comics have been showin' up since six, begging for a spot."

Morty disappeared down behind the bar for a second and it sounded as if he was horkin' up a Chevy. He came back up and started filling bowls with peanuts while he puffed his cigar, staring me down. "Either the rats around here are getting bigger, or the comedians are getting smaller."

"No, this here's my kid, boss," Dad said, grabbing a handful of nuts. "He's visiting me for the weekend."

"Well, he'd better be twenty-one and real short for his age, see, or I could lose my license."

"I just turned twelve," I told him.

"Well, don't advertise it!" Morty barked, slamming the bar. "For cryin' out loud, Teddy, didn't you teach him any sense?"

Dad was crunching away on the nuts and went for another handful. "Would it be okay if I snuck him backstage, so he can see me do my set from the wings? The kid'll get a real kick out of it."

Sweet!

"Just keep it on the down low," Morty grumbled, "or it's *my* butt that'll be in a sling." I tried to picture that for a second, but decided it was just a weird expression.

"I owe ya one, boss."

Morty snubbed out the burning end of his cigar, blew on

it, then slid it into his shirt pocket without flinching. "I tell ya, the things I let you clowns get away with."

Literally, in Dad's case.

He led me through the dark, noisy club to a place called the greenroom where the comedians waited to go on. I hear every theatre has one, too – this was my *first*, which was a real thrill. Funny, because it wasn't green at all – more like flesh-colored. Rotting flesh. Still, I was stoked getting to be around all these authentic show-biz folks. From their reactions when we walked in, you could tell that everyone knew Dad. He wet some cocktail napkins at the sink and started scrubbing off his makeup while he introduced me one by one.

There were too many for their names to sink in, but the ones that stuck were Jack Wackerly, the Wacky Wonder of Wacker Drive; Willy Wong (at first I thought he'd said Willy Wonka); and my favorite of the nut cluster, Ruby Ray – or as she put it: "Ruby, like the gem; and Ray, like a drop of pure sunshine." She was a large, black woman polishing off a liter of Diet Shasta. Instead of shaking my hand like the rest of them, she shook my jaw and said, "Mmm, look at that sweet, young face. Ruby Ray's got her some toothbrushes older than that face!"

A narrow door marked MEN-WOMEN-UNDECIDED opened a crack and a guy's gravelly voice said, "Anybody got any dried leaves? Morty still hasn't sprung for a roll of toilet paper, that cheap son of a –"

"Lenny!" Dad interrupted. "My son is here. Remember, I told you guys he was coming? His name's Dustin."

"Yeah? Like Dustin Hoffman, the famous actor?" An eyeball appeared in the crack. "Are you a famous actor too?"

"Kinda," I mumbled. I hated that I was coming off all shy and self-conscious. That totally wasn't like me. "Definitely!"

"Nice to meet ya." He extended his hand out the bathroom door – like he actually wanted me to shake it. I handed him the packet of tissues that Mom had stuffed into my pocket, followed by the bottle of hand sanitizer. I swear, it was as if she could predict the future.

"Lenny, you got no class!" Ruby yelled, slamming the door on his arm. Lenny yowled. "How many times we got to tell you to keep that door shut when you're doin' your business?"

"It's cool," I said. "I'm not too grossed out – my gran does the same thing all the time."

Everybody got a big kick out of that. Miss Ruby grabbed my hand and dragged me onto the duct-taped couch next to Willy Wong, who was wearing a Bart Simpson T-shirt. Either he was in deep meditation or passed out cold. "Now hold this nice and steady for me, baby, so I can reapply my face," she said, handing me a tiny, chipped pocket mirror. "Tonight Ruby Ray's gonna get discovered – I can feel it in my bones. My *funny* bones."

I sat holding the mirror, watching Dad pace back and forth, while Ruby added another layer of makeup to the one she already had on. There was a preshow buzz of excitement filling the air and I found myself buzzing right along with everyone else. The whole thing reminded me of backstage at Buttermilk Falls Elementary before opening night. Only these guys were the real deal – show-biz folk living their dream. It was exhilarating being surrounded by my "peeps!"

"So, Teddy," the Wacky Wonder said, digging through his box of props, "are we gonna finally get to meet Shelly tonight too?"

"What? Nah, not tonight," Dad answered. "She's back at the apartment."

My stomach did a flip-flop. I almost fumbled the mirror.

"Haven't you kept that doll to yourself long enough?" Lenny said from the john.

"Yeah, Teddy," Ruby added. "You been talking about her for the last two months, but we ain't seen hide nor hair of her. Now my mama didn't raise no fool. Is she for real or are you just making her up?"

Oh, gawd, please let him be making her up! Another woman? I hadn't even considered that. How were my parents supposed to magically get back together with *her* in the way? *What if they're married already? What if she makes me call her Mother?*

"Where's Teddy?" Morty barged into the greenroom chewing his putrid cigar. "There ya are. I hate to do this to ya with your kid here and all, but I'm gonna have to bump ya from the lineup tonight. Gary Glass just walked in the door – someone must've tipped him off about the talent scout." (Ruby yelled out something I can't repeat.) "You're low man on the totem pole and he's my biggest draw. Sorry, but dem's the breaks."

Practically all the comics in the room offered Dad their spots, but he passed – said it wasn't fair. Not only was he a stand-up comic, he was a real stand-up guy.

"Just for the record, I think this stinks," I told him on our way out of the club.

"You heard the man, 'Dem's the breaks,'" he said, imitating Morty's rasp. He was acting like it didn't bug him, but I knew different. "Those talent scouts show up all the time but I don't know of a single person who's been discovered yet."

On the bleak ride to Dad's apartment, one burning question kept swirling around in my head like Morty's cigar smoke: "Who's Shelly?" But it never escaped my lips.

Chapter 11

Peanut Butter and Shelly

There were so many flights of stairs leading up to Dad's apartment, by the time we got there I had jet lag. I leaned breathlessly against the banister, listening to babies screeching, while Dad unlocked the seventy-five locks on his dented door.

"Home, sweet home." Dad rammed the door open with his shoulder and flipped on the light switch. "Now I know it ain't exactly the Ritz . . ."

That was being too kind. It was barely bigger than a Ritz cracker. And the décor was – I guess you'd call it shabby chic, only without the chic. It looked like Gordy's room on a bad day. Squalor I believe is the word Mom uses to describe it. Wait, let me think. *Gordon, how can you sleep surrounded by such squalor?* Yeah, squalor.

"Lemme give you the grand tour," Dad said through his

bullhorn as if I were a crowd of fifty. "This here is the great room; over there's the john. And that concludes the grand tour!" We threw our jackets on an overloaded coatrack, toppling it over. "I know it's a dump, but like I said, it's just temporary."

Temporary seemed to be a permanent feature when it came to Dad.

"So sit down, take a load off." He jiggled my shoulders. "Rel*aaa*x!"

How could I relax? I kept expecting that home wrecker, Shelly, to come rushing into the room any second in skimpy lingerie and bunny slippers.

"You could throw your stuff anywhere."

That seemed to be the general rule. I dropped my backpack and looked around the not-so-great room for somewhere to sit. Dad cleared a pizza box off a beat-up armchair and I collapsed into it – the chair, not the box. A cloud of dust actually puffed up from the cushion.

"Sorry I didn't have time to pick up," Dad said, rushing around scooping up handfuls of stuff. "I was running late." He disappeared into the bathroom and came back a second later empty-handed. Still no Shelly. "So what can I do ya for? You want anything to eat – drink?" I shrugged. "Don't get bashful on me now. I know my cupboard's not completely bare ..." Dad was going for the cabinet, but veered off to the window instead, and pulled down the shade with a quick jerk. "Which is more than I can say for my next-door neighbor!"

That could've used a "bah-*dum*-pum," but I was too busy picking at a cigarette burn in the armrest and having a panic attack.

"Let's see what's on the menu," he said, opening the cabinet. "Peanut butter, creamy; peanut butter, crunchy; and peanut butter, all natural – for the discriminating palate."

"What about Shelly?" I blurted out.

He just kept rummaging.

"I'm really sorry to have to break this to you, kid," he said turning to me. *Brace yourself – here comes the bomb.* "But I'm all outta jelly."

"Shelly!" I practically screamed.

"Oh. How did you find out about Shelly?"

"At the Laugheteria – hello? Your friends were teasing you about her right in front of me."

"Oh, right, right, right."

His brain was as scattered as his dirty laundry.

"Well," he said with a wiggly worm of a smile, "wanna meet her?"

Let's not and say we did. "Okay."

"Just sit tight," he told me, rushing to the other side of the room. "Don't go anywhere."

Where would I go?

Dad wrenched open a warped closet door and a bunch of shoe boxes and junk spilled out on top of him. He shoved it all back in except for a black leather case – kind of like Wally's bassoon case, only bigger – then ran out the front door of the apartment, closing it behind him.

Where's he off to? Is he coming back? I knew I was being ridiculous, but I still couldn't help wondering. I perused the room, trying to spot his phone just in case I had to call Mom to come and rescue me. After all, Dad had a reputation for running away when things got weird.

Buzz!

I jumped. That had to be the loudest doorbell in the history of doorbells.

"Dad?" I said, rushing to the door.

Buzz-buzz-buzzz! Knock-knock-knock!

"C'mon, quit screwing around!"

I twisted the doorknob and pulled the door open. Nobody there. When I stuck my head around the door frame, a big purple thing lunged out at me.

"*Eeesh!*" I yelped. "What the –?"

"You must be Dustin," it said in a high, tinny voice. "I'm Shelly. Nice to make your acquaintance."

A ventriloquist dummy? Who would've guessed I'd be so stoked to meet a three-foot-tall purple mermaid puppet? She had turquoise hair with starfish stuck in it, a long, floppy tail, and two sparkly shells where a bikini top would be.

"I'd shake your hand, kid, but mine are all *clammy*. Bah-*dum*-pum!"

"Dad! I knew you were up to something – *fishy*."

"He's a real cutie, Ted," he went on à la Shelly. "Too bad I'm dating a Navy Seal."

"Oh, gawd."

Dad unclenched his jaw and switched to his real voice. "Well, whaddya think? Ain't she something? Ask her how old she is, Dusty. Go ahead, ask."

"*Daaad,* can we take this inside?"

"C'mon, throw me a *line*. Just for the *halibut*."

"All right already. I'll *bite*."

"Ha! That's m'boy!"

"So, Shelly, what year were you – spawned?"

"Lemme think . . . I can't remember the exact date. But the Dead Sea was just starting to get sick!"

I pulled Dad and company into the apartment before the neighbors called the men in the white coats.

"What did the Pacific Ocean say to the Atlantic?"

This was getting old real quick. I was drowning in fish jokes! Plus, he was really bad at keeping his lips from moving. Still, I was so relieved that Shelly wasn't a real live woman, I just kept playing along.

"I don't know. What *did* the Pacific say to the Atlantic?"

"Nothing. It just waved."

I threw myself across the couch in exhaustion.

"Okay, folks, that's my time." Dad must've gotten the hint. Shelly took her curtain call (with help from Dad, of course) and wound up propped on the couch next to me.

"Give it up for the comic stylings of Teddy Grubbs and Shelly!" I shouted, tossing a pillow into the air. I was clapping and whistling on the outside, but on the inside I was thinking, *If that's his new act, he's in real trouble.*

"Uh-oh, speaking of time," Dad said, glaring at his watch, "I gotta drop my cab off by nine o'clock or I'll be in deep doodoo." He rushed to the dresser across the room and started digging through the bottom drawer like a maniac.

"You never did tell me how your audition for the school musical went. I definitely want the play-by-play when I get back, okay, buddy?"

I got a *sinking* feeling.

"Here, this oughta keep you entertained till I get back," he said, shoving a videotape into the VCR/DVD combo next to the small TV atop the dresser.

"What is it?" Please don't let it be *The Little Mermaid*.

"You'll find out." He tossed me the remote. "The taxi hub is just around the corner, so I'll be back faster than you can say Jack Robinson."

"Jack Robinson."

"A thousand times." He grabbed his jacket and shot out the door with a wink.

Once again my heart froze in my chest. I guess it was, like, a Pavlov-and-his-dogs type thing. I ran to the door and locked it because I was in the big city and you just can't be too careful; then curled up on the couch next to "the other woman."

"So, home wrecker, shall we *dive* right in? Whaddya say?" I clicked on the TV with the remote.

"*. . . hear it again for Miss Thompson's first-grade snow angels and Santa's little helpers.*" The sound blasted out, but the picture was still fuzz. "*Good job. You really knocked it outta the park!*" There was clapping and cheering, then Mr. Futterman appeared on the screen! This must've been from a long time ago because he still had a patch of hair. "*And now Mrs. Sternhagen's second-graders will present a Christmas recitation, followed by a festive song of the season.*"

Mrs. Sternhagen waved her students onstage, and waddled down the steps to the piano. I swear she was wearing the same brown dress she had on last week.

"Oh, I know what this is," I said out loud to Shelly. "The Christmas pageant from five years ago that we had at our school." I squeezed the contraption in Shelly's back that worked her mouth, answering myself in a high falsetto. "I know a family of clownfish that travels around in a *school*."

"*Shhh!* Watch the movie. Hey, look, that's me! In front of the leaning Christmas tree, carrying the letter *S*. Jeez, my head was gi-normous!"

The nine of us with speaking parts and placards were like

bumper cars trying to find our spots in the CHRISTMAS lineup. First we spelled out SHIRTSCAM; then CRASHMIST; then THISCRAMS. Pretty funny! The audience seemed to think so too.

Finally we ended up in the correct boy-girl-boy-girl positions. Sternhagen was barking something at us. "Now I want to see expressions of joy on your little faces or there will be serious consequences!" I'm guessing. She cued us to begin and the first kid stepped forward to recite his line.

"*C* is for the CAROLS that we sing from days of old – yore!"

"*H* is for the HOLLY WREATH that hangs upon the door,"

Gee, I wonder why Holly Peterson got that line.

"*R* is for the REINDEER that guide Santa's special sleigh,"

"*I* is for the, uh, ICICLES that – umm, shimmer – no glimmer . . ."

Millicent Fleener was freaking out, flipping the placard around like she thought she was holding it upside down. Didn't matter – it was an *I*!

This is painful. I fast-forwarded it.

"– the ANGELS bright,"

"And *S* is for the SNOW!" a mini-Dustin hollered.

Applause, applause. We all took an awkward bow and the other letters marched off to their places on the chorus bleachers joining the rest of our class. But not me. I stayed put and just kept on bowing away. Beaming. Mugging.

Then it hit me. "Omigod!" I cried out, pointing at the

screen. "That's it! The exact moment in time when I knew I wanted to be an actor! Six little words and I was hooked."

Shelly seemed unimpressed. But I was flying high. I pressed REWIND and PLAY to see it again. "– S is for the SNOW!" And again, and again. What a find! A major turning point of my life caught on tape. They could play it to embarrass me when I'm a big star promoting my latest movie on Leno and Letterman. "Oh, no!" I'll gasp, pretending to be mortified, but loving every minute. "Now where the heck did you dig that up?"

Dad came barging through the front door coughing, wheezing and breaking my time-travel spell. "I'm back!"

"Jack Robinson, Jack Robinson. *Whew!* Nine hundred and ninety-nine. You made it by the skin of your teeth!" He didn't get it. "Dad, this tape is so cool. I didn't know you had it."

"Don't tell your mother – she'll want it back." He fell onto the couch, reeking of cigarette smoke, and stretched his legs across me. "She just called my cell," he said, kicking off a shoe. His big toe was poking through his sock, staring up at me. "Said to remind you that she'll be picking you up at the Greyhound bus station on Sunday at six sharp."

"How can I forget? She embroidered it into the tags of all my shirts."

My second-grade class launched into "Holly Jolly Christmas" with full arm choreography and we both zeroed in on the TV. "Oh, look, there's my little guy!" Dad gushed. The camera panned in on my adorable (I have to admit) face. "Hey, did you forget the words to the song or something? Look close. You're not even moving your lips."

"Which is more than I can say for you." Okay – I didn't really say it out loud.

"See? See? I never noticed that before." He scooched upright to get a better view. "Maybe ventriloquism runs in the family, huh?"

"Nope. That's 'cause I was a Hummingbird," I said proudly. Dad had a question-mark look on his face. "I remember – Sternhagen had a few of us hum along instead of singing. She called us the Hummingbirds. We were – special."

"Oh, okay."

As I heard myself saying the words, it dawned on me what a total goofball I'd been. My excitement fizzled. The Hummingbirds were special all right – especially *bad*. We weren't even allowed to sing along with the rest of the class, and they weren't exactly the Mormon Tabernacle Choir. I'd been duped!

What if I haven't improved at all since then? What if I wasn't just having an off day when I auditioned for the musical? What if I was born with some sort of incurable singing impairment?

"Okay, time to get off me, Pops. Your legs weigh a ton." *What if, what if, what if?* I clicked off the TV. My hummingbird feathers were definitely ruffled.

"I gotta pee like a racehorse anyway." He rolled to his feet and darted toward the bathroom, calling out, "We can order some real food if you're hungry. There're menus on the coffee table."

"What coffee table?"

"One man's milk crate is another man's coffee table. Smart aleck."

Shuffling through the take-out menus, I kept thinking about how I'd turned out to be one of those people who *thinks* they can sing, but really can't, and go around making gigantic goobers of themselves. *How depressing.* I caught myself humming a sad rendition of the stupid "Holly Jolly" song and bit my lip. *I'll never be able to look another hummingbird in the beak again!*

"I can't believe I fell for it hook, line, and sinker," I said out loud, turning to Shelly. "Uh, you can use that line in your act if you want."

Just when I had the restaurants narrowed down to Tex-Mex Express and Wok-the-Talk, I heard a muffled *riiing!* coming from under my left buttock.

"Hey, Dad, the couch is ringing!" I yelled, feeling between the cushions for something shaped like a phone. "It's probably Mom checking up on me again."

"Well, get it!"

I almost answered a checkbook, a banana, and a statuette of the Sears Tower before I got to Dad's cell phone.

"Hello, hello?" I said, flipping open the phone. "Uh, Grubbs residence."

"*Teddy? It's Nadine Fleck. I'm so glad I caught you.*"

Dad was still doing up his pants when he leaned out of the bathroom asking, "Who is it, Dusty?"

"A Dean Frick?" I threw him the phone and he actually pulled off a one-handed catch.

"That's Nadine, my agent," he told me in a stage whisper, covering the phone. "She never calls."

Dad was knocking over glasses, struggling to jot stuff down on a roll of paper towels during their conversation. It was over quick, and he flipped the phone closed with a resounding "Yes!" and flew into the living room. "Well, kid, I've got good news – and I've got *good* news." Sunbeams were pouring out of his eye sockets. "Which do you want to hear first?"

"Umm, the good news."

"Your father has an audition for a national television commercial tomorrow morning! Can you believe it?"

"Sweet! And the *good* news?"

"You get to tag along!"

Chapter 12

Stink-Zappers

Dad took a slow, hard drag out of his cigarette, savoring it as if he were sucking on the straw of the last chocolate milkshake on Earth. He flicked it onto Wabash Avenue without thinking twice. And without thinking twice, I stomped on it, snatched it up and dropped it into a nearby trash can.

"I could learn a few things from you, pal," he said, smiling. And with our arms around each other we monkey-walked into the glassy, green high-rise that housed McKenna Casting, Inc. The chrome elevator was rocket-ship fast and we only made one stop on our ascent to the forty-seventh floor. I think my stomach got off with the cleaning lady on thirty-one. When the elevator doors opened, all we saw was the Prestige Modeling Agency.

"This can't be right." Dad looked as confused as the supermodel he was holding the elevator door open for. He didn't notice that I'd noticed, but he was staring at her like she was Little Red Riding Hood dipped in gravy and he was the wolf.

"Yeah, the casting office is definitely on forty-seven," I said, pulling him away from the elevator. "Hey, Dad, did you know most penguins mate for life?"

"Where did that come from?"

It was a cheap shot, but a kid's gotta do what a kid's gotta do. As we were speed-walking past Prestige, I spotted a CLOSED FOR REMODELING sign on their door. "Oh, look," I said, pointing it out, "Do you think that means they're hiring all new models – or just fixing up the place?"

Dad didn't react at first. Then he busted out laughing as if it were the most hilarious thing he'd ever heard. "You're a funny kid, Dustin. Don't ever let anyone tell you you're not funny."

"I won't."

It turned out that McKenna Casting, Inc. was at the opposite end of the hall behind a giant glass door. Dad had to sign in at the reception desk, where a silver-haired lady snapped his picture and handed him a large index card. "You can take a seat over there with the others and . . ." she said, but her voice petered out. "You'll be reading for the role of . . ."

"Excuse me?" Dad asked, leaning into her. She was one of those real soft talkers who should only be allowed to work in libraries.

"The role of Smelly Father," she repeated. "I'll give you your sides."

"Sides?" I half-expected her to whip out a dish of coleslaw, fries, or creamed spinach – but she removed a few typed pages from a file folder and handed them to Dad.

He flipped through the pages as we walked past a lineup of chairs filled with a variety of anxious-looking people devouring their own sides. "It's, like, the script," Dad muttered, "I guess."

"Smelly Father – you're perfect for the part! I can't believe we're in a *real* casting agency, and you're up for a *real* commercial. How exciting is this?"

"Exciting? Jeez, Louise, I think I'm having a coronary. I'm sure glad I got my lucky charm with me."

"What is it, like, a rabbit's foot or something?"

"No, it's *you,* dum-dum. I thought my agent had crossed me off her list. You show up and – *bam!* I'm auditioning for my first national commercial."

We took off our jackets and plopped down on two orange fuzzy chairs. Dad was filling out his information card and I noticed that his button-down was totally wrinkled. In fact, he was way underdressed compared to his competition – and he still had sheet marks across his cheek. *Real classy.* Maybe that would work in his favor, though, since he looked more like a smelly father than the other guys.

"Lemme see." I grabbed the sides from him and read his

lines out loud. "'Honey, I'm home! Rough day today. My dogs are really barkin'.' I don't get it. What's this commercial for? Pet food?"

"Stink-Zapper Insoles, you know, for the insides of your shoes. Just three lines, that's not bad. I suppose I should memorize them, huh?"

"Definitely! Get them cemented in your brain and then I'll test you."

I spotted one of the boys, roughly my age, staring a hole through my forehead. I smiled at him. He didn't smile back. Some of the other Smelly Fathers were mouthing their lines and gesturing to the empty air. If it didn't say McKenna Casting, Inc. on the door, you'd have thought we were in the waiting room at the loony bin.

"Honey, I'm home. Rough dog today – *dang it!*" Dad rehearsed, swatting the paper. "Gawd, I'm a wreck. I wish I could smoke in here."

"Don't," I warned. "Take deep breaths, it'll help you relax. And if you screw up, just launch into a joke or something. Remember, funny never fails."

"That advice sounds real familiar. I guess the shoe's on the other foot now."

"But I wouldn't suggest the water-drinking thing. That one kind of backfired on me," I said. "Okay, keep working on your lines, Pop, I'll be right back."

I dashed over to the vending machine in the lobby and

bought a box of lemon candies. Dad smelled like an ashtray and I didn't want the casting people holding that against him. I popped one into my mouth on the way back. "Here ya go. My treat," I said, dropping the box onto Dad's lap. "Holy mackerel, these things're sour."

The double doors behind the reception desk sprung open and a boy rushed out. "I totally nailed it!" he spouted, zooming over to a woman sitting across from us.

"I'm talking painfully sour," I stressed, sucking away. "*Sow-er!*"

"So spit it out," Dad told me.

"But they're also strangely addictive."

"Sylvia, why are these agents sending us pretty boys?" a large man said, bursting through the same double doors. He had a goatee or a Vandyke – whatever those minibeards are called. "Didn't I say I needed quirky for this commercial? Quirky-quirky-quirky!"

"You approved every single name on the list. And I ... no way of knowing ..." Sylvia's voice was fading in and out again, as Goatee Man leaned against the doorjamb massaging his temples. "... when they show up in person."

"But they don't look at all like the pictures their agents faxed over!" The man put on a pair of square glasses, pushed up the sleeves of his multicolor sweater, and peered into the waiting room. "Let's see, how many boys do we have left? One, two – four?"

"Just three," Sylvia replied, checking her clipboard.

"Okay, maybe it's my new trifocals, but I'm counting four."

I bit into the core of the lemon drop and got a burst of sourness that sent tears squirting out my eyes. My whole head turned into one giant pucker and I finally had to spit the darn thing out. But the damage was done: fuzzy tongue and itchy tonsils. *They should put a warning label on these things.* I wiggled a finger in my ear and was forcing air down my throat to scratch the unreachable itch. But I must've been grunting too loudly because I noticed Sylvia pointing at me.

"That one's not an actor," I heard her say.

I object!

"But look at him – that's Nerdy Boy!"

The Goatee Man's eyes widened like he'd just spotted Bigfoot. He scurried toward me. I almost ran.

"Hello, young man," he chirped, looking down at me. I untwisted my face and sat up straight. "I'm Mr. Weiss. Nathan Weiss. I'm directing the Stink-Zappers commercial. And you are?"

Freaking out!

"Mr. Grubbs. Dustin Grubbs. Uh, I'm here with my Smelly Father – uh, my dad."

"Honey, I'm home. Rough day today. My dogs are really barkin'," Dad recited proudly.

"Not yet. We'll call you when it's time," Mr. Weiss said, never taking his eyes off yours truly. "So, Dustin, you're exactly the type we're looking for. Would you by any chance be at all interesting in auditioning for our television commercial today? That is, if it's okay with your father."

"Huh?" *Did he just say those words or am I dreaming?*

"Okay by me," Dad said, looking stunned. "Go for it!"

"Well?" Mr. Weiss was waiting for my answer. I couldn't move. "Dustin? What's it gonna be?"

"Yeah, sure! *Definitely!*"

"Fantastic. Come with me."

"Right now?"

I sprang up to my feet so fast I got dizzy. Dad might've said "Break a leg, kid," but all I could hear for sure was the blood rushing to my head. *God, no one back home will ever believe it! I might have just been "discovered," which Dad said never happened in reality – just in old movie musicals. This was, like, a zillion times better than some school play – this was the real deal.*

"Excuse me, sir, but will I get a chance to look over my lines first?" I asked, following Mr. Weiss through the waiting room. It felt as if I were wading through water with hams strapped to my ankles.

"No lines," he told me. "Just be you."

But there are a bunch of me's. Happy me; bummed-out me; goofball me; don't-mess-with-me me. Which one do they want? Probably not terrified, sick-to-my-stomach me – even though that's the real me at the moment. Suddenly I couldn't swallow. Or breathe. Just my luck I'd drop dead before I reached the audition room.

"But my Kyle is supposed to be up next!" a loud woman complained to Sylvia as we passed the reception desk. "This is outrageous. I'll have you know he was the spokesbaby for Li'l Darlin' Disposable Diapers."

"I'll alert the media," Mr. Weiss said dryly and ushered me through the double doors. "We're gonna need a Polaroid of this one, Syl. And more coffee – gallons of it."

The next thing I knew I was facing a firing squad of three very bored looking people sitting behind a foldout table. I couldn't feel my tongue. I think I was having a nervous breakdown.

"Here's our next victim, guys. Dustin Grubbs," Mr. Weiss said, perching on the table. Everybody perked up. "He's not on the roster, but he's perfect, don't you think? He belongs to one of our Smelly Fathers."

"Hi." I gave them a flat wave, trying desperately to steady my trembling legs.

"Marvelous – Offbeat – Interesting," they said at the same time. "Deliciously ordinary, but in an extraordinary way."

"One look at that face and you immediately think – *boom* – Stink-Zapper Insoles!" the younger woman added. She was staring at me so intensely I thought for sure I had something disgusting dangling from my nose. "So, Dustin, how old are you? Have you done any acting before?"

"Twelve – just turned. I starred in our school play last year out in Buttermilk Falls."

Once again they were jabbering over one another. I heard the word "confident" bleed through, and "Reads younger – Very green." I quickly brushed my wrist across my nostrils.

The older lady asked, "Oh, so you don't reside here in Chicago?" and pursed her bright red lips.

I probably should've left out the Buttermilk Falls part.

"No, ma'am. Just visiting my dad for the weekend."

"Do you have any experience in front of a camera – at all?" a man with a mouthful of bagel asked. He had his feet on the table with his chair tipped back against the wall.

"Uh –"

I considered lying for a nanosecond, but I knew I wasn't a good liar. *Wait! I don't have to lie.*

"As a matter of fact, my brother shot some recent footage of me singing in the shower. Umm – but I'm not willing to do nude scenes."

"Quick – Funny – Good answer," they said with a collective chuckle. "Sharp as a tack."

"Okay, let's get down to the nitty-gritty," Mr. Weiss said, whipping off his glasses and moving to a tall director's chair. "The commercial spot is for Stink-Zapper Insoles." He waggled a floppy, blue gel-filled shoe stuffer in front of him, then tossed it onto the table with a *thwack*.

"Uh-huh, I'm familiar." I nodded enthusiastically. "I love those things!"

"They're not on the market yet. But I applaud your enthusiasm."

They all got a real hoot out of that. I decided to keep my piehole shut unless absolutely necessary.

"Let me give you a quick scenario of the commercial," Mr. Weiss went on. "Your father comes home from a hard day at work, kicks off his shoes, and his feet really smell something awful, see? Rancid, like a stink bomb just went off. Then the camera pans in on the flowers wilting, the dog's ears standing straight up, and you – his son, making a hilariously funny face and passing out on the floor. You get me?"

"I think so. Shoes, stink, face, fall."

"And don't be afraid to take it over the top," he added.

Meaning?

"Right," the young woman agreed. "You can't go too far."

I mulled that one over for a second.

"Uh, does that mean I'm not *allowed* to go too far," I asked, "or, like, the farther the better? Should I –"

Mr. Weiss interrupted with, "Why don't you start out on the stool?"

"The latter," the lady said.

Now I was totally confused. I turned around and walked over to where they were pointing. There wasn't any ladder, but there was a stool, so I hopped onto it. *Shoes-face-stink-fall. That ain't it.*

"Just FYI," Mr. Weiss said, "we're putting your audition on tape so we could review it later. Robbie, start the camera rolling."

I could see my face bouncing around on the monitor atop a tall, metal stand against the wall. This was so cool. *Another defining milestone being captured on tape! I wonder if I could order copies.*

"Whenever you're ready," Mr. Weiss said, leaning forward. "Eyes to camera, state your name, then show us what you've got."

The big, black camera setup, complete with a long boom mic bobbing over my head, looked like something out of *Star Wars.* I stared cross-eyed at the small, red light over the camera lens and flashed my pearly whites.

"Give us your name," Mr. Weiss reminded me.

"Oh, yeah. Umm . . . uh . . ." *Cripes!* "Don't tell me –"

"Dustin Grubbs!" he yelled.

"Dustin Grubbs!"

"And action!"

Now what? I folded my arms to keep my heart from lurching out of my chest. For some reason that stupid Christmas-pageant line I'd had in second grade popped into my head: *And S is for the snow!* I was clearly cracking up. *Concentrate, Grubbs. Snow-shoes-face-fall. No, wait!*

Luckily, Mr. Weiss started giving me direction.

"You're lounging in your living room – your dad enters. 'Honey, I'm home . . . rough day,' blah-blah-blah . . . he kicks off his shoes and you catch wind of it . . ."

His words distorted into distant gibberish. All I remember after that was making a goofy face and falling off the stool.

"Huh," Mr. Weiss said with a deadpan expression. No one else uttered a word, but their eyeballs were jumping from one to the other like Ping-Pong Balls.

I scrambled back onto the stool, expecting to take it from the top a bunch more times. (An actor rarely gets it right on the first take.) But after some whispering at the table, the bagel guy told me, "That's all we need for today." The same exact words I got from Miss Honeywell after my *Oliver!* audition. Not a good sign. I just wanted to make a quick exit. "Thank you for your time," I murmured and opened the doors to the waiting room. Sylvia immediately snapped a Polaroid picture of me and handed me a form to fill out. My legs were wobbly as licorice sticks as I hurried over to Dad and fell into my chair in a heap.

"Well?" he asked, studying my face. "Did you knock their socks off?"

"Not exactly." I tried blinking away the spots I was seeing from the camera flash; tried figuring out what had just happened. "It all went by so fast."

"Well, chalk it up to experience. You've got your first big, professional audition under your belt now. Not too shabby. How many sixth-graders could say that?"

"Dad, I'm in seventh."

I was still catching my breath from the overwhelmingness of the whole thing when the double doors flew open and Robbie, the cameraman, sprinted over to me.

"Dustin Grubbs, right? They need to talk to you for a second."

I locked eyes with Dad. No words were uttered but we could read each other's thought bubbles. They both said:

"!!!"

Chapter 13

Doberdoodle Down

I followed Robbie back into the audition room and stood in exactly the same spot I was three minutes earlier. The casting team was staring at me with Shelly-the-Mermaid's unblinking eyes. Heart clattering. Stomach mooing like a sick cow. My body was making such a racket, I moved right up to the table so I wouldn't miss a word.

"First off," Mr. Weiss, said, "all of us agree that you gave a dynamite audition. I just wanted to let you know that. There's something real special about you – charm, charisma, whatever you wanna call it. And the camera just loves you."

"Thanks," I squeaked, totally flabbergasted. "I love it right back."

Okay, cut to the chase – where do I sign? Quick, before I pass out.

"That being said, McKenna Casting, Inc. has certain policies and procedures we must adhere to. And this is a highly unusual situation – what with you having no experience, no representation, and being in town for just a few days."

Uh-oh!

"And so, Dustin, under the circumstances . . ."

Don't bust out crying when he finishes that sentence.

". . . we'd like to schedule a callback for you on the spot."

"Beg pardon?"

"Do you think you can arrange to be back in Chicago on October eighth? All the top execs from Stink-Zappers will be here to make the final cuts. I think it falls on a Saturday."

"But I clean out my fish tank on Saturdays," I almost said just as a joke. I decided not to risk it. "Yeah, sure. Absolutely. Count on it!"

Fireworks were going off inside me. I'm talking bottle rockets, M80s, Roman candles. I was surprised my ears weren't smoking.

"Super. See Sylvia at the front desk and she'll set up a time and give you the necessary info." Mr. Weiss finished. I'd floated halfway out the door, but he waved me back into the room. "Listen, son," he said in a half-whisper, "we realize your father is auditioning for this thing too, and that can get a bit awkward. So we'll try to get back to his agent with a yea or nay ASAP. And we'll see you on October eighth. Deal?"

"Deal! Thank you so much!" I gushed, pumping his hand, and worked my way down the table. "And *you* . . . and *you* . . . and *you* . . ."

Dad was totally blown away when I told him the news. Couldn't even speak at first. Then a "Wow!" blurted out of him and he smothered me in a bear hug. "I'm so proud of you, kid!"

"You're cutting off my air supply!"

He backed off for a second, then hugged me again. "That means we'll get to spend another weekend together. That's what they call a win-win situation."

"Hey, Dad, what if we *both* get cast?" I asked, settling down in my chair. "It could happen! I mean it'd make sense. They're looking for a father and son, and we're a *real* father and son. We could make a whole series of commercials, then tour the country promoting Stink-Zappers. How cool would that be?"

Dad sat back and gave me an arched eyebrow for his answer. The same eyebrow I used to get whenever I asked stupid questions like, "If Santa sets off the burglar alarm, they can't throw him in prison for breaking and entering, can they?"

He popped another lemon torture-drop into his mouth and said he needed a few quiet moments so he could get himself together before they called him in. I was too excited to sit still. Granny always said if she could bottle my excess energy, she'd sell it and make a fortune. At the moment I could fill a ten-ton drum and still have enough steam to cartwheel my way back to Buttermilk Falls.

I completed the McKenna Casting, Inc. form and handed it back to Sylvia. On my way back to my seat I picked up the *Highlights* magazine just as she called out, "Theodore Grubbs . . . up next . . . and follow me." But before I could spot the teapot in the pumpkin patch, Dad's audition was over.

"Quick and painless," he muttered, grabbing his jacket off the chair next to me. "C'mon, kid, let's make like a tree and leave."

Dad was totally convinced that he'd screwed up his audition, so I couldn't exactly be kicking up my heels in front of him, celebrating my incredible news. Not unless his agent called with some incredible news of his own. We traipsed around Marshall Field's Department Store for a while devouring obscene amounts of Frango Mints, but Dad's cell phone didn't ring once. We took in two centuries' worth of paintings at the Art Institute, but Dad's cell phone didn't ring once. We stuffed our faces with four courses of Chinese food, but – okay, halfway through our Happy Family on a Sizzling Plate he got a wrong number, but other than that, the lousy phone didn't ring once. I was a pupu platter of emotions during the rest of dinner. And when our fortune cookies came (I was "born with shining star above head"; Dad's was blank) – let's just say our dinner at Shanghai Five didn't exactly end in high fives.

Early the next morning, Dad and I awoke to the long-awaited ring. Finally! But by the time he'd found the phone and answered it, his agent had already hung up, having left the following message:

"Teddy? Hi, it's Nadine Fleck. I heard back from the McKenna Casting people – unfortunately, they're gonna pass. No callback, sorry. Get this, they said you weren't believable as a father! Craziness, right? Personally, I think they were looking for a different type altogether. I understand they're really interested in your son, though, so I guess it wasn't a complete loss. Listen, maybe you'd like to bring him by the office sometime –"

Dad was supposed to drop me off at the Greyhound bus station in his cab, but he must've really needed the company because he decided he'd drive me all the way to Buttermilk Falls instead. That meant suppressing my joy bubbles for almost two hours – which would probably cause permanent damage to my spleen or something, but it was the least I could do. He was so bummed out. "Not believable as a father" – that had to sting.

"I'm really sorry," I said, "about – you know."

"Par for the course. But I'm bustin' with pride about my boy. Really. I am." Dad lit up a cigarette and cracked his window open for the smoke to escape. "Yeah, my stand-up career hasn't exactly been – a career, if you catch my drift." I caught it. I also caught a lungful of cigarette smoke and started hacking big time. "Oh, for the love of –" He rolled the window all the way down and flicked out his cigarette; then reached over and pulled the zipper of my jacket all the way up.

We drove in silence through town after town, and I took to counting cows to calm myself as the sky turned a deep pumpkin color with a magenta border. It had been such a rainy, white haze of a day, who would've expected such a finale? I was beginning to get mesmerized by the endless string of telephone lines whizzing by, when out of the clear blue – uh, pumpkin – sky:

"You know, I miss you and your brother. A lot. Your mother too. And Olive, and Birdie – even Granny. Don't be surprised if I end up back in Buttermilk Falls someday soon with my pride stuffed in a suitcase." *Whoa. What?* I turned to look at his face – he seemed dead serious. "Your gran would probably greet me with a stiff uppercut, and I wouldn't blame her. But she'd come around eventually."

I could picture Granny doing the uppercut thing but I couldn't see her doing the coming around thing. Still, with Dad talking about moving back home, my joy bubbles were out of control. *I might explode like a shaken seltzer bottle!*

"I'm forty-six years old," he went on, stopping at a red light, "maybe it's about time I grew up. At this point in my life I could use a little normal."

Just as he said those words I looked out the window – and cross my heart and hope to spit, there was a big, gold sign that read WELCOME TO NORMAL. You can't make this stuff up!

Maybe Dad wasn't the greatest stand-up comedian, or ventriloquist, or (God knows) parent, but his timing was spot on – you had to give him that. I took a second look and noticed something move. It was black and furry. And I think it was peeing on the sign. One blink later and it had collapsed onto the grass. So much for normal.

"Omigod!" I cried. "Did you see that?"

"What?"

"Pull over quick! I think it's a dog – and he's hurt!"

Dad spun the steering wheel and we squealed to the side of the road. Both of us flew from the taxi to the whining dog, who seemed happy to see us – but definitely in pain. And very wet.

"Nice, doggy," I muttered, cautiously kneeling at his side. "Shoot! No collar."

"And look. His back leg is really messed up," Dad said, wincing. "Must've gotten sideswiped by a car, poor pooch. He's lucky he's alive."

We carefully lifted the dog into the back of the cab, where he gave himself a clumsy shake, drenching me and the entire seat. I was doing my best to quickly sop up the water with Dad's clown wig when the dog kind of collapsed onto me. I held him on my lap, gently stroking his quivering body. "Hold on, boy," I whispered over his constant whimpering. "You're gonna be okay."

Dad switched on the overhead light, quickly called

Information on his cell phone, and got the number of a veterinarian who had a home office on the outskirts of Normal. But halfway through the vet's directions the phone ran out of juice.

"Don't worry, kid, I'll find it," Dad assured me, tossing the phone on the dash and stepping on the gas. "We'll be there in a jiffy."

The dog was breathing really fast now and licking blood off his back leg, which was obviously in bad shape. He was a very strange-looking dog. Kind of resembled a giant poodle, but with a Doberman pinscher's head.

"Cripes, you know who he looks like? Shatzi!"

"Who?"

"Our principal's doberdoodle – the mascot for the basketball team. Come to think of it, I saw a missing-dog flier up at school – but it was all marked up, I could barely read it."

I examined the dog's back closely and noticed the slight imprint of the *F* for Fireballs that Futterman had shaved into his fur for the final game of last season. This was definite proof. What were the chances?

"Hang in there, Shatzi," I murmured, petting him gently. His heartbeat was off the charts – vibrating through my hand. "Gawd, are we almost there?"

"I think so. But it's getting darker by the minute and it's tough to read the signs. Keep your eyes peeled for Pigeon Forge Road."

I squinted out the window but all I saw was me squinting back. Suddenly it seemed awfully quiet. Shatzi's whimpering had stopped.

"Oh, no. *Dad?* I don't think he's breathing right – or at all." My throat tightened. "Shatzi? *Shatzi?*" I said, rocking him gently. No sign of life. "Dad, he's not moving. What am I supposed to do?"

"Do you know CPR?"

"No! I don't even know what it stands for. Culinary Precipitation – something."

"Just wing it. Breathe into his mouth – and massage his chest, I guess."

"*What*? I haven't even gone that far with a *girl*. Dad, you do it!"

"I can't drive and do CPR at the same time."

"Taxi!" someone yelled, stepping off the curb. The cab swerved and I banged my head on the door.

"*Oww!*"

"Jerk!" Dad yelled through his window. "Can't you see I'm not for hire?"

I had to pull myself together. Fast! *The only way I'm gonna get through this is to psych myself out,* I thought, my temples throbbing. *I'm an actor, right? I can do anything if I'm playing a character. Okay, I'm filming my big scene from – I don't know –* ER: Special Canine Unit.

"Talk me through the procedure," I said out loud with

shaky determination. "I'm ready to administer mouth-to-mouth."

"Isn't it more like mouth-to-snout?"

"Dad!"

"Sorry. Okay, just breathe slowly into his mouth. And give it a three-count –"

In my mind I had become renowned veterinarian, Dr. Dorian Sinclair, and without wasting another second, I planted my lips on Shatzi's, cupped my hands around his muzzle, and blew.

"Wait. Gross!" I pulled away. "His breath smells like – *ugh*, he must've just eaten one of his doodies." *Call in the stunt double.*

"Don't stop!" Dad insisted, glaring at me via the rearview mirror. "Find your rhythm and stick to it."

Take two! I transformed back into Dr. Sinclair again – holding my nose and blowing, rubbing, and gagging for what seemed like fifteen minutes. I might have imagined it, but I think I heard Dad mumbling that his gas gauge was almost on empty. That's when panic officially kicked in. This was turning into one of those action sequences where everything goes from bad to worse – and the next thing you know people are throwing words around like *Jaws of Life* and *medevac*."

"Any change yet?" I heard from the driver's seat.

I came up for air and did a quick scan of the dog's body.

"Don't think so. Gawd," I said, brushing the hair out of my eyes, "I'm kinda poopin' out."

"Just keep at it, kid!"

Take three! I put muzzle back to muzzle and gave it my all. My head felt like a giant pincushion and I knew I was running out of time and – like the taxicab, gas. Just as I was about to give up, Dad announced, "We're here! Pigeon Forge Road." *Hallelujah!* He made a sudden, sharp turn and Shatzi rolled half off my lap.

"Oh, no! D*aaa*d!"

As I was struggling to pull the dog back up I heard a kind of muffled snort. Then a sneeze. And then, miracle of miracles, I saw two pointy ears twitching and a puffy tail wag. Dr. Sinclair fell back into his seat, hyperventilating but relieved. And with breath that could stun a moose.

Cut! Print! Emmy!

Chapter 14

Fisticuffs

"Thank God!" Mom gushed, smothering me in an eager hug. Suddenly she held me at arm's length, squeezing my shoulders. "I'm so angry I could shake you." It was a Dr. Jekyll-Mr. Hyde moment for sure. "You're forty-five minutes late! Get in that car. *Now!*"

"But, Mom," I pleaded, "you don't understand –"

"No 'but, Moms.' I said now!"

I threw myself into the passenger seat and she slammed the car door.

"I was at my wit's end, Ted!" she raved, stomping over to Dad's cab. "Waiting in this godforsaken Greyhound bus parking lot without so much as a dime phone call."

"A *dime?*" I questioned from the car window.

"Dustin, don't!" she warned.

"We would've called, but Dad's cell phone pooped out."

Her rage was too thick for my words to cut through. I

hadn't seen her so mad since their predivorce knockdown drag outs.

"I didn't know whether he'd missed the bus, or was kidnapped – or lying dead in the street somewhere!"

"There's a perfectly good explanation, Dorothy," Dad said quietly, reaching out the window for her hand, "if you'll just calm down for a second."

"Don't tell me to calm down!" She pulled her arm away and backed up from the taxi. "And to think I was finally beginning to trust you again . . ."

Conversation over. Mom got back into her Hyundai and we tore out of the lot, knocking over a garbage can. I turned and watched the blue LuvQUEST.com sign on Dad's cab getting smaller and smaller while I waited for the smoke in Mom's head to clear.

"His explanation *is* pretty solid," I told her. "Trust me."

"I don't want to hear it."

But I told her anyway. I could actually see the anger slowly draining from Mom's face as I went through all the details.

"You guys are heroes," she uttered, finally back to being her usual composed self. "Poor Shatzi. Is he going to be all right?"

"Yeah, no broken bones. Just lacerated ligaments or something. We told the vet we were in a real hurry, so he promised he'd get a hold of Futterman to come pick up the dog."

"I feel just awful now, after the tongue-lashing I gave your father. But I'll make it up to him – I will." *Okay by me!* Mom leaned over and planted one on my cheek. "Oooh," she said, wrinkling her nose. "Honey."

"What is it?"

"Why don't you grab yourself a handful of Tic tacs from my purse?"

By the time we pulled into the driveway, I'd filled Mom in on my Stink-Zappers audition and she flipped out all over again. But this time in a good way. She couldn't wait to get into the house – chomping at the bit to brag about her famous son to the family, no doubt. *Break out the spray cheese and crackers, 'cause we've got more celebrating to do!* And I was right behind her crunching through the leaves, flying up the porch steps, zooming past Wally, bursting through –

Wait! *Zooming past Wally?*

"Well, look who it is!" I plopped down on the top step next to him. "My best friend in the world, waiting to welcome me home from my trip." *And without the Oxymoron.*

"I wasn't exactly waiting."

"Oh. Then what're you doin' here?"

"This." Wally held up a crumply tissue with a gnarled pipe cleaner sticking out of it. "I was just pedaling by and your aunt Birdie recruited me into helping make fake carnations for the wedding. She wouldn't take 'Oww, you're hurting my arm' for an answer. Everyone's in the kitchen, but it's nuts in there."

"That's supposed to be a flower?"

"Here, take over – this is your job anyway." He dumped his supplies onto my lap and rolled to his feet. "I've gotta trek, 'cause Les is gonna help me figure out our repertoire for Opus Five. My quintet is a go! I'm so stoked. We've even booked our first real gig!"

"Cool," I said coolly.

"Plus, he just got the new Deutsche Gramophone recording of Bartok's Divertimento for Strings."

All I heard was blah-dee-blah-dee-blah – strings.

"C'mon, man, can't you stick around for, like, five minutes?" I whined. "You're gonna drop dead when you hear what happened to me!"

Suddenly I heard "Push it! Push it!" coming from down the street. I could only hope someone wasn't giving birth on their front lawn. You never know with Buttermilk Fallians. "Harder! How bad do you want it?"

It was Mr. Kincaid barking orders at Zack, who was jogging along Chugwater Road. Backward. Zack looked miserable – all purple and wheezing. I think the gigantic backpack he was wearing must've been loaded with anvils. He stopped to take a quick hit off his asthma inhaler, and trudged on. *Man, how bad* did *he want it?*

"No wonder Zack acts like such a sludge ball," I muttered.

Wally waited for them to pass, then hopped down the stairs and mounted his bike – that same lame girl's bike he was riding before. "Okay, see ya, wouldn't wanna be ya."

Hard to believe puberty was knocking at his door.

"Alrighty then. I guess you don't wanna hear how I got discovered by a major casting agency in Chicago. You've probably got better things to do than listen to me blab about my first professional audition – for a television commercial – that'll be aired nationwide – and in some parts of Canada!"

"Oh, yeah?" he said, barely raising an eyebrow. "Cool."

"I know, right? They set up a callback for me on the spot, which they *never* do – for Saturday, October eighth . . ." But Wally started pedaling away into the leafy, dark shadows. "They said I've got charisma!" I shouted after him. "That the camera loves me!" No response. *Major dis!* "Hey, call me later, okay?"

"You call me."

"No, *you* call *me!*"

I strutted into the downstairs kitchen to Aunt Olive's announcement of "Here's our star!" and a rush of applause. *Now that's more like it.* "Your mom tells us you took Chicago by storm. Bravo!"

"Tell us every little detail of your big-time audition!" Aunt Birdie cried.

I gave them the *CliffsNotes* version, but included four full reenactments of my much-acclaimed falling-off-the-stool-from-the-overwhelming-shoe-stink moment. After a standing ovation, I was plucked from the heights of glory and swiftly recruited into the flower-making crew. The table was buried in an avalanche of white tissue carnations, which were going to be used to decorate the newlyweds' getaway station wagon. How many did they need? We already had enough to cover a float for the Macy's Thanksgiving Day Parade.

"I wanna hear all about your visit with Teddy too," Aunt Olive whispered excitedly across the table. "Later. When anny-Gray's ot-nay ere-hay."

Aunt Birdie took a second to decode, then nodded in agreement and went back to folding her ten-thousandth tissue. "I'm thinking of getting some buttocks on my face," she said matter-of-factly. "So I look nice for the wedding."

Mom and Aunt Olive stopped midfold and turned to her with puzzled squints.

"You know, those shots – like all the celebrities get?"

Aunt Birdie wasn't exactly the brightest bulb in the marquee. But I've learned over time that if you just roll around what she says in your brain for a little while, you'll come up with what she really means.

"Botox!" I blurted out.

"Isn't that what I said?"

Everyone laughed so hard that half the fake flowers got blown onto the floor. Cinnamon woke from her nap next to the radiator and was in instant kitty heaven batting at the carnations. The room got even rowdier when she started zooming laps around the table with a flower dangling from her mouth.

"Don't let me interrupt your shindig, I'm just here for a banana," Granny said, shuffling into the kitchen. "You'd better clean up this mess when you're through and I'm not gonna say it twice. We're starting to get bugs." Instant party poopage. She bent over to pick up a single carnation – in agony, of course. "Oh, sweet Moses, my arthritis."

"Just leave them, Ma, for heaven's sake," Aunt Olive said impatiently. "And no one gets bugs in October from leaving tissues around."

"Bugs!" Granny insisted, banging the flower on the table. "I still don't think you've got your head screwed on straight, lady, with all this wedding hooey. But you're a grown woman and you can do as you darn well please."

I grabbed a banana from the fruit bowl on the counter and presented it to my gran as if she were the Queen of England. "'Ere ya go, m'lady," I said, breaking into my cockney accent to lighten the mood. *The consummate showman – able to slip into character in the blink of an eye.* "Got a nice ripe one 'ere for ya. Fancy that!" She grabbed the banana with a grunt. "Feelin' a bit cheeky today, are we, love?"

"Dustin, quit your playacting and come with me," Granny ordered. She hobbled her way past Gordy, who was barreling into the kitchen. "That screwy postman mixed in some of your mail with ours again. I could box his ears!"

"What, fisticuffs?" Gordy said, punching the air.

I froze. That was one of the Artful Dodger's lines from *Oliver!* It means a fistfight – I'd looked it up. Gordy was groping through the fruit bowl on the counter when he noticed my questioning glare.

"What?" he snarled. "It's a real word!" He took a sloppy bite of an apple and put it right back in the bowl. "It's on that lame CD you've been playing on a loop for the last two weeks."

That makes sense, I guess. Seeing our two worlds collide there for a brief second kinda threw me.

Sifting through the stack of mail on the dining room credenza, I got to thinking about how I was still looking forward to being onstage again, even though my television career was taking off like gangbusters. *I could end up being a filthy-rich movie star someday, but I shall always return to my humble roots in the theatre!* Suddenly I felt Gordy's dragon breath on my neck as I separated silver-trimmed wedding RSVPs from bills addressed to Mom; magazines addressed to Mom; a letter addressed to Mr. Gordon Grubbs – *from NBC Studios?*

"Why the heck are you getting mail from NBC?" I asked, whipping my head around. "What're you not telling me? Huh?"

Brother Grimm tore the envelope away from me and took off with a knuckle-punch to my arm. Right on cue Cinnamon leaped out of nowhere, latching onto his back in an all-out attack. *"Aaargh!"* Gordy howled, flailing and twisting down the hall. "Get this mangy thing off me!"

I used to think cats were minions of the Devil, but this one was beginning to grow on me. Back to the mail – and another stupid postcard from LMNOP.

Hi, Dustin Grubbs,
What's up? Are you giving Cinnamon lots of sweet kisses? Went whale watching today and saw a pod of humpbacks! Incredibly awesome!!! I nearly froze to death, though, and ended up "losing my lunch" in Stellwagen Bank.

Too much information!

"All right, stop dillydallying and bring those wedding cards to your aunt." Granny gave me an impatient push. "Get 'em outta my sight."

I was about to head back to flower central when my own words stopped me.

"Gran, why are you acting like this?" She refused to look up – just kept smoothing out the lace doily on the credenza. *Someone has to talk some sense into her before she drives us all up the wall.* "Aunt Olive said she'd still send you money every month and come visit every chance she gets."

"Oh, you don't know nothin'," Granny groused, waving away my words. "You're just a snot-nosed kid."

I dropped the mail and blew my nose on one of the tissue carnations that were peppered all around. "There ya go," I said, tossing it over my shoulder. "Snot free. So why don't you educate me then?" I grabbed her hand and led her to the "sweet spot" on the living room sofa, her favorite seat in the house. Granny zeroed in on peeling her banana, sniffing it and taking a careful first bite.

"You want some?" she offered. "It's good if you have the runs."

"I don't have the – spill it, Gran."

"What do you want me to say? I didn't expect your aunt to abandon us, running off with that bug killer . . ." She was beginning to open up, but somehow veered off track, going on and on about the noisy garbage trucks waking up the whole neighborhood.

"Hello? Earth to Granny! We were talking about Aunt Olive."

"Yeah, yeah, use your indoor voice." She closed up the peels on what was left of her banana and set it on her lap. "For your information I brought up all that wedding baloney in the confessional at St. Agatha's yesterday – to that young Father Downing."

"And? What'd he say?"

"Nothin' worth a darn. He's got this *holier than thou* attitude."

"I give up!" I hollered, springing to my feet. The heat of frustration was burning my face as I bolted to the credenza and grabbed the stack of mail. "You wanna know what I think?"

"No."

"I think you're just gonna miss Aunt Olive. A lot! And that's all there is to it. I know *I* am."

"Looks like somebody's gotten too big for his own britches." She flung the banana across the coffee table, knocking off the pink poodle figurine. "Next, you'll be moving away to the big city, just like your father. You think I don't know where you've been this weekend? Well, I *do*."

I'd had it. I stomped back into the kitchen before we got into a bloody round of fisticuffs! Everyone had gone but Aunt Olive, who was stuffing carnations into huge plastic bags. "Oh, Dustin, would you be a love and go through those response cards and record the 'accepts' and 'regrets' in my wedding journal? I'm up to my elbows in flowers."

"No sweat." She cleared a spot for me at the table, and I got to work. There weren't many invited guests, just close family and friends, so things were sailing right along. It wasn't until I'd gotten to Great-Aunt Iris's RSVP that I'd actually stopped and read one of the things. It wasn't until I'd gotten to Great-Aunt Iris's RSVP that I couldn't breathe.

We look forward to celebrating with you on . . . Just like in some demented Disney cartoon, the swirly-curly wedding date jumped off the card, spun through the air, and singed my eyeballs:

Saturday, the eighth of October

Chapter 15

The After Math Aftermath

"You have reached the offices of McKenna Casting, Inc. If you know the party you wish to speak to, please say their name now."

"Nathan Weiss."

"Rachel White. If this is correct, press the pound key. If not, please repeat the name of the party you wish to speak to."

"Na-than Weiss."

"Donald Baumgartner. If this is correct . . ."

Argh! I had no choice but to stay on the line to speak to a human operator, who finally connected me to Mr. Weiss. Naturally he wasn't in, so I left a voice mail.

"Oh, yeah, hi. This is Dustin Grubbs – the actor from Buttermilk Falls. Uh, I have a callback for the Stink-Zappers commercial at one-forty on October eighth, but that's not good for me so I'd like to change that, please. To another day. Any day. Halloween even. I have to leave for school now, but I can be reached anytime after three-thirty. Okay, thanks. Bye."

I'd decided before the first school bell rang that I wasn't going to let Aunt Olive know just yet that she went and picked the worst possible day of the year to get hitched. Didn't want her getting all worried for nothing. This was just a minor glitch, and I knew I'd be able to work it all out – or die trying. In the meantime, I couldn't wait to saturate the entire playground with my "True Hollywood Story." Pepper was psyched when I told her and she insisted I autograph her sweatshirt with a Sharpie. My best friend, on the other hand, was nowhere to be found.

Once we were trapped inside Lynch's lair, my sense of celebrity quickly fizzled out. Culture shock, I guess. I'd gone from a whirlwind weekend of show-biz glamour and big city razzmatazz to a grueling morning of dividing compound fractions. *Bleah.* Mom must've dropped me on my head as a baby and damaged the math side of my brain because it never came easily. And slave-driver Lynch had six of us lined up elbow-to-elbow along the lengthy chalkboard at the back of the room, working out problems in a display of public humiliation. What was the point? Stars of TV commercials hired teams of accountants to divide their fractions *for* them.

"Miss Wathom, this may well be the biggest cranberry muffin I've ever seen – and it smells heavenly." Mr. Lynch was peeling back the plastic wrap and drooling over the thing as he paraded past me. It was hard enough to concentrate, being math impaired, without mouthwatering distractions. "I'll exercise some restraint and wait until lunchtime," he oozed on. "Tell your mother she's outdone herself this time. But please get control of your hair, dear, so Mr. Ziggler can see the board."

Dear? Maggie's suck-up routine seemed to be working. She had been smothering Lynch with baked goods ever since she discovered he had a major say in the casting of the musical. We'll see if the kitchen closes after the cast list goes up.

"Mr. Grubbs, everyone else appears to be finished," Lynch said, setting the megamuffin on his desk with a thud. "Is there a problem?"

"Not really." I was staring at my denominator so hard the numbers disappeared. *Focus, Grubbs. Divide and conquer.* "I take that back. It's kind of the problem that's the problem. I just don't get it."

"Well, let's break it down. Why don't you start out by refreshing the class's memory on the rules for converting compound fractions to simple fractions?"

"'Appy to oblige, gov-nah!" Cockney again. It just popped out of me when I least expected it. I faced the class and saw Maggie looking up at me, pulling her frizzy curls into a ponytail the size of a tumbleweed. "Okay, the rules for converting compound fractions." I cracked my knuckles. "Now correct me if I'm wrong, but I'm guessing it's not '*I* before *E* except after *C*.'"

Candy giggled. That was when I first noticed it. SLUDGE was

printed across her hot pink T-shirt in gold glitter. *Hmm. Why is that word so familiar?* I stood there twiddling a fat piece of chalk, trying to shift my thoughts back to fraction rules, but my eyes jumped to Pig. He was wearing the same shirt too, only in brown with white letters. And Tyler had an orange one with black letters. I scoured the room and realized half the class was wearing those shirts. Green, blue, yellow – SLUDGE, SLUDGE, SLUDGE. There was a sudden twinge in the pit of my stomach. I smelled something foul – and not just Stewy's macrobiotic fish balls.

"Well, Mr. Grubbs?" Lynch's voice cut through my wandering thoughts. "Do you know the answer or not?"

"Yes. No. Wait – what was the question again?"

"Take your seat," he said all disgusted. "You're wasting our time with your tomfoolery."

Clearly I wasn't racking up any brownie points with the Lynch-man – and after my disastrous *Oliver!* audition I needed all the help I could get. I mean how would it look if the star of a TV commercial with all kinds of natural-born charisma didn't even get a decent part in his own school play? I'd be the laughingstock of the Screen Actors Guild. I was certainly feeling the pressure – what with that wedding-date conflict eating away at me all morning, and now the whole SLUDGE thing. I had to find out what the deal was with that before I'd completely cracked up.

It wasn't until around elevenish, when my class was

independently working on our Shedd Aquarium reports and Lynch was noisily printing stuff out on his computer, that I had my chance. I was about to ask Candy "What's with the shirts?" when she turned her head slightly and whispered, "Don't hate me," through a veil of hair.

"Okay. But why would I –"

"For telling Zack. That you called him sludge. Well, him and the Fireballs." She was talking in camouflaged sound bites so Lynch wouldn't catch on. "You remember. At the Shedd?"

"Uh, kinda."

"It sorta just slipped out. Zack's my boyfriend now, so . . ."

Ouch! Pepper gave me a constipated look from two rows down. She was right – Candy really *had* been drooling over that boneheaded Neanderthal the whole time. Candy went back to working on her report, nervously twisting her tresses over one shoulder. The message that was suddenly revealed on the back of her shirt made the SLUDGE thing pretty clear:

Sports
Lovers
Unite!
Drama
Geeks
Bit**E**!

Seems like the jocks had taken my snide remark and practically turned it into an all-out battle cry. Lynch was making a racket rummaging through his supply closet and the printer was still coughing out page after page, so I took that opportunity to drag Candy through the mud.

"Well, that was a chintzy thing to do, snitching on me like that," I whispered. "You cheated on the acronym, by the way. 'Drama Geeks Bite'? Pretty slack. More like a slack-ronym."

"Poetic license."

"Yeah? Yours should be revoked."

"C'mon, Dustin, don't hate me." She turned all the way around to face me. Her eyelids were hot pink to match her shirt. "Zack's dad is on a rampage – it was his idea to have the shirts printed up. He thinks the athletes really need to take a stand before they all get swallowed up by the artsy-fartsy freaks. His words, not mine."

"That's the stupidest thing I've ever heard. Hard to believe you got sucked in by that crowd."

"Is it? Don't you remember my nickname last year?" I tried to think, but drew a blank. I'd barely noticed her back then. "Stale Candy. Well, look at me now. Suddenly I'm sitting at the cool girls' table at lunch; suddenly I'm on the cheerleader squad and dating the captain of the Fireballs. Suddenly I'm cashews, pecans, and almonds dipped in chocolate with a creamy caramel center!"

She's nuts all right.

The room got quiet again. Lynch was back at his desk stapling stuff and undressing his cranberry muffin with his eyes – so we had no choice but to get back to our aquarium reports. I made an executive decision right then to change my topic from "Penguins: Just the Facts in Black and White" to

POISONOUS FROGS: THE PRETTIER, THE DEADLIER!

Beware of the beautiful dart frogs! They may look real tasty, but looks can be ~~decieving~~ – deceiving. Their bright colors serve as a warning to potential predators

The loudspeaker clicked on, derailing my train of thought, and Futterman's voice came ringing through. "Sorry I'm late with my morning announcements – *cough-cough* – but I'm battling a nasty head cold today. I spent the entire weekend searching for my dog in the freezing rain. Thankfully, he's home safe and sound."

Shatzi! I'm glad he's okay.

"Let's see, the first item on the agenda ... the Slam-Dunk Basketball Tournament we were subbosed to be hosting at our school this year will be held at Claymore Middle School in Lotustown again. Sorry, guys. No big explanation, except that our facilities didn't beasure up."

"So it's official!" Tyler blurted out through an eruption of moans and groans.

"Also, Coach Mockler will be on a short leave of absence starting – abbarently, last Wednesday." A few kids gasped. "In the beantime, Miss Blodget will be taking over his gym classes as well as the bractice sessions for the Fireballs."

"That cow?" someone yelled. "No way!"

"We're doomed!" Pig snarled, pounding his desk. The rest of the SLUDGE-wearers went ballistic. I'm talking booing, hissing, and gnashing of teeth.

"People, people!" Lynch lurched. "I won't have this behavior in my classroom!"

"Settle down, everyone," Futterman said, as if he could magically hear the uproar too. "I'm sure this will all be worked out. Eventually." That brought things down to a simmering grumble. "Oh, just one bore thing. The Arts Committee has wrapped up their final auditions at Fenton High, and the cast list for *Oliver!* will be posted ASA" – *gross, wet nose-blowing* – "P."

Lynch was in a crabby mood for the rest of the day. And as if the war brewing around us wasn't bad enough, he assigned us four Civil War chapters to read for homework, plus a five-page essay of our choice on the Battle of Gettysburg, the Battle of Fredericksburg, or the Battle of Shiloh. I guess that's what they mean by picking your battles. Not very *civil* if you ask me. But I wasn't about to let anything rain on my parade.

Not Lynch, not Candy, not the clump of SLUDGE-wearing Fireballs tearing up the school grounds at three-fifteen.

I hid behind the monkey bars until they dispersed, then sprinted all the way home. Perfect timing! I could hear our upstairs kitchen phone ringing as I rumbled up the porch steps.

"Hello? Hello?" I was still panting like a choo-choo train when I answered it.

"Justine Grubbs?"

"Dustin Grubbs – yes, speaking!"

"Oh, that's a D? This is Sylvia LeRoy from McKenna Casting, Inc. I'm afraid I have some bad news."

Chapter 16

Pande-phone-ium

WARNING: TITLE CHARACTER'S HEAD MAY EXPLODE DURING THE FOLLOWING TELEPHONE CONVERSATION. PLEASE PROCEED READING WITH EXTREME CAUTION!

"Are you still there, Mr. Grubbs?"

"I'm here. Sorry, I just had to grab onto something."

"Oh, uh-huh. I'm calling to acknowledge that we did receive your message earlier today about a scheduling conflict, but I'm afraid . . . only one day of callbacks . . . October eighth."

Shoot! It was that gray-haired lady whose voice always fades out.

"Excuse me? Only one day did you say?"

"Yes."

No!

"The Stink-Zapper executives will be flying in . . . only going to

be here for just that one Saturday . . . *final decision on casting their commercial.*

"Oh, man." I could barely speak – but I *had* to. "Well, do you think – can I maybe get an earlier time slot? It's super-important or I wouldn't even ask. See, my aunt is getting married at two o'clock that day. I could still make it down to Chicago and back in time – but the trip takes a couple hours, so any time before noon would work for me. Any time at all – ten, nine, eight, seven, six –"

"I'm afraid that's impossible. We're booked solid."

"But – then – can't I just switch times with someone?"

"We make it a policy never to do that. These are professional . . . very busy lives . . . can't just rearrange their schedules willy-nilly."

Freaking out on my end. Brain working a million miles a minute. Heart too.

"Hello? Mr. Grubbs?"

"Umm. I could get, like, a written excuse from my mom, if you want – or my doctor. Or my priest! Whatever it takes."

"We're not running a grade school here, honey – although some-times it seems like it. [BEEP] . . . the real world. Oh, I'm getting another call. Can you hold for a sec?"

You've gotta be kidding me! It was the longest, gnarliest "sec" since the beginning of time. I kept pick-pick-picking at the loose corner of the apple wallpaper border until it looked more like apple brown Betty.

"*Sorry. It's our busiest time of day . . . always happens. Now which agency did you say you were with again?*"

"Uh, I didn't. No agency. Just me, Dustin Grubbs, remember?"

"*Oh, right, of course. Yes, we're going to need a definite answer from you before the week is out. If you can't make it . . . us know as soon as possible so we can arrange for another actor to fill your time slot, okay? [BEEP] Oh, I apologize, but I really have to take this other [BEEP] . . .*"

"Yes, ma'am," I said all polite. "Thank you very much for –"
But she'd already hung up.

I slammed down the phone and shook my fists at the heavens. "This is not happening! This is totally whacked out!"

Why I started revving up the can opener on the kitchen counter after that is anybody's guess – but I couldn't stop. The *grrrr* sound must've matched how I felt inside. *Okay, easy, cowboy. Just calm down. Aunt Olive would definitely understand if I skipped out on her wedding for something this huge, right? Right.* "Grrrrrrr!" *She's a reasonable woman, right? Right. So just suck it up and lay it on the line.* I backed away from the can opener, turned to the sink, and splashed some cold water on my face. *You mean right now?* I asked myself. *The sooner the better.*

I meandered down the back steps with Cinnamon nudging my ankles from behind. Sometimes I wondered whether that cat wasn't really LMNOP in disguise. Aunt Olive was in the kitchen winding up a phone call of her own – to the bug man no doubt.

"Thanks, Pookie Bear, for doing this. I'm sure he'll be thrilled." She dropped her volume way down when she saw Granny approaching. "Yes, until tomorrow night then. I'll miss you," she cooed. "No, I'll miss *you* more! No, *I'll* miss –"

Granny grabbed the receiver from her and barked into it, "Meet my friend, Click!" and hung up the phone.

It was pretty funny, but I was too frenzied to laugh. My aunt didn't get upset either – in fact, she seemed really excited about something. "Oh, just the guy I'm looking for. Wait'll I tell you – you're gonna flip!" *My thoughts exactly.* She pulled me into the walk-in pantry to get out of earshot of Granny, and closed the door. "Now this doesn't compare to your TV commercial – not even close," she said, opening a bag of Oreos and stuffing one into her mouth. "But I know from personal experience – *crunch* – that nothing can beat the thrill of entertaining a live crowd." *Crunch-crunch.* "Am I right? Cookie?"

"No."

"No?" she asked, chewing.

"No to the cookie part." *Just be direct.* "*Grrrr.*" "Listen, Aunt Olive, I have something really imp –"

"Your grandmother leaves these goodies lying around on

purpose like booby traps. For spite. She knows I still have a few more pounds to shed before the wedding."

"Piece-a-cake."

"Where?" Aunt Olive asked, scanning the shelves.

"I meant easy. But you know ... if you changed it to a spring wedding, you'd have plenty of time to slim down. And there'd be roses on that trellis out back instead of dead vines. Something to think about."

So much for being direct.

"Don't be silly, we couldn't possibly postpone the date. The RSVPs have already been returned," she said through chocolate-stained teeth. "Not to mention nonrefundable deposits on the cake, and the caterers, and the priest –"

"People can be very understanding," I lied. "Or you know what would be cool? Eloping! Flying off to Vegas and having, like, an Elvis-themed wedding."

I was definitely on a roll!

"Okay, now I know you're razzing me. Being surrounded by family at my wedding means the world to me, you know that. I couldn't imagine getting married without seeing your smiling face – right there." It got quiet for a minute. Aunt Olive hid the Oreos behind a giant can of sunflower oil, then turned to me with sad eyes. *Not the sad eyes!* "You realize we're not going to be seeing as much of each other anymore, you and I," she whispered. "Not after I move away to Hinkleyville."

Ooh, didn't see that one coming. I almost launched into the auto-response of "Sure we will. You'll visit us – we'll visit you," but I stopped myself. Even if it turned out to be true, things were never going to be the same. She was dead right. In an awkward moment of not knowing what to say I ripped into a nearby bag of minimarshmallows and shoved a fistful into my mouth.

"Anyway, what was I talking about? Oh! The promotion for my Dennis's new business. He was going on about hiring an actor through a talent agency to hand out fliers in a funny costume at the Hinkleyville Mall. Well, that set off a bell in my head! I told him, 'You call them right back and cancel, because I have the perfect guy for the job.' So? Are you interested?"

"Oh, I don't think I could –"

"It pays seventy-five bucks."

"– pass up an opportunity like that. Thanks for pulling for me."

Not exactly the acting role of a lifetime, but how could I say no? Aunt Olive grabbed a box of Ding Dongs off a shelf and we were done. Mission aborted. I'd officially chickened out.

It's not over till it's over, I told myself, leaving a marshmallow trail on the way upstairs, *or until the fat lady sings.* But when I reached the top landing, "I'm getting married in the mooorning . . ." came wafting up in Aunt Olive's wobbly soprano. It was a sign.

Operation desperation! There had to be another way. *Maybe I should tackle the whole thing from a different angle?* But there weren't any more angles. I figured I'd call Dad – he's always full of advice – he'd know what to do. But when I picked up the phone again, my brother's voice came squawking through the receiver.

"No, Becca, not the song from the karaoke bar. I just rocked out to a Foo Fighters tune – but they really ate it up. Yeah, for real! They said they were lookin' for a guy like me with a good strong voice who could –"

"Sorry, Gord, but you have to hang up right now. I've got a real emergency."

"Get off the freakin' phone, you nosy, little –"

Why can't we have our own separate phone lines like civilized people? I had to regroup, organize my thoughts, and really kick things into high gear. Desperate situations called for working things out with a pen and paper – for some reason that always helped. So I made a mad dash to my room to equip myself with stationery, then hauled butt back downstairs again for a series of frantic phone calls. Luckily, no one was hanging out in the kitchen and their telephone was *(whew!)* available.

Here are the final results as recorded in my spiral notebook:

<u>Call #1: Dad.</u> (Collect.) Totally weirded out. Will check with agent to see if she can

"pull some strings" for me! I'm not supposed
to count on anything, though.
<u>Call #2: Wally.</u> (Mrs. Dorkin answered.) Not
home. At Oxymoron's house and gonna spend
the night. Figures! Why did I even bother?
<u>Call #3: Pepper.</u> Freaked when I told her.
Said I should try bribing casting people, like
Maggie was doing to Lynch with baked goods.
Brilliant idea! But did I want to sink to
Maggie's level of butter-uppery? YES!
Pepper's suggestion: Send them a basket
of minimuffins. Too blah.

Flowers? Balloons maybe? A box of chocolates? No, no –
and definitely nothing to do with candy. I ran up to my room
and searched around on the Internet for the next, like, two
hours until I came up with a real winner. Ballads-to-Go! *I
could appeal to their sense of theatrics.* They only took credit
cards, though, so I had to drag Mom into the picture when
she got home from work.

"Oh, Dustin, you're going a little overboard, don't you
think? I'm happy to put it on my card for you, but – I'll have
to eventually get reimbursed."

So I *burst* open my piggy bank and forked over every last
cent of the $138.73 of birthday money it was digesting. I did

have that mall job coming up so what the heck? Spare no expense, right? I mean this was my life we were talking about!

Cutting to the chase, here's how it was supposed to go down. Picture it: ten AM Wednesday morning, Uncle Sam flies into the front office at McKenna Casting, Inc. and shouts, "*I want you* – to change Dustin Grubbs's time slot!" Then to the tune of "Yankee Doodle" he belts out my original singing telegram:

"Have a heart and don't make Dustin forfeit his audition
He would sooner eat a rat than be in that position.
Dustin Grubbs is talented. Dustin Grubbs is funny.
He'll be perfect for the part and make you tons of money!"

Chapter 17

Malled

I'd thought it was genius, but so far the Uncle-Sam-O-Gram had been a total bust. Friday had come and gone and I hadn't heard jack from McKenna Casting, Inc. If they didn't leave a message by the time I got home from my mall gig on Saturday, I'd have to call them and – I don't know what. Offer up my firstborn child?

It was barely October, so the Hinkleyville Mall should've been decorated for Halloween. Instead, it looked as if it had been attacked by Santa's Elves. They'd decked the mall with boughs of fake holly, visions of inedible sugarplums, and one hulking Styrofoam snowman. Mr. Smashum stationed me on the second floor next to a mirrored pillar, opposite Hickory Farms. His only instructions to me were, "If anyone asks, you're sixteen." So there I stood – just me in a spongy Tommy the Termite costume and a box of fliers. I was Dustin Grubbs: One-Man Bug.

"Twenty dollars off," I mumbled to the passersby, holding out a limp flier. No takers, just a lot of strange looks. At least I was miles outside of Buttermilk Falls, where people didn't know me. I mean I had a reputation to protect, and this was at the bottom of the show-biz ladder – one rung up from being a mime.

All right, if you're gonna do this thing, give it all you've got. I adjusted the airplane-size wings that were scratching my neck and took a deep breath of smoked meats and cheeses. "Yowza-yowza-yowza! Smashum Brothers Pest Control is offering twenty bucks off your next exterminating job. That's twenty – two, zero American dollars. Step right up, folks. You don't wanna pass up this amazing offer!"

"Oh, look, sweetie," a lady said, pointing me out to her sticky-faced little girl. "A big butterfly."

"Termite, actually. Take a flier?"

As I was handing her one, her little brat gave me a swift kick in the shins and took off running.

"*Oww*, that hurt! Bugs have feelings too, ya know!"

I saw red. Not rage – hair. Pepper, her mother, and her baby sister were passing the bug molesters, headed my way. What were the chances? Five minutes on the job and I wanted to file for unemployment.

"Dustin?" Pepper did a triple take. I'd never actually seen one before. "Hey! Is that you? What's with the getup?" she asked, swatting my antenna. "You in the Witness Protection Program or something?"

"I don't know what that means. Just doing a favor for my aunt's fiancé – but I *am* getting paid. What are you guys doing out here?"

"What's all of Buttermilk Falls doing here?" Pepper's mom said, wiping a string of drool off the baby's mouth. "It's the Shop-Early-Shop-Smart Pre-Christmas Extravaganza Sale!"

"You're kidding?"

"It's huge! We already got such a deal on towels at Bergmann's Department Store." She started maneuvering through an army of Old Navy bags loaded in the back of the stroller. "My sister does makeovers in their cosmetics department, so we got her employee discount on top of the sale price," she blabbed on, pulling out the corner of a plain, blue towel from a Bergmann's bag. "Look. Twelve-ninety-nine for real Egyptian cotton!"

"Very absorbent," I felt obliged to say.

She rearranged the bags and proceeded to unzip her long, puffy coat, hardly coming up for air. "So, big shot, Pepper tells us you might be in a real TV commercial. That's really something. You excited?"

"Yep." *Quick change of subject.* "That the baby? Man, she's grown."

"That's my li'l puddin', Joy-Noelle." She hoisted the kid out of her stroller and rested her on her hip. "Well, not so little. Nine pounds, twelve ounces coming out the chute."

"Gawd, Mom! Spare us the grimy details."

The baby fit right in with the whole holiday theme. Having been born on December twenty-fourth, they slapped one of those Christmassy names on her. I guess Carol was too plain. It's a good thing it wasn't a boy or he could've wound up being a Rudolph – or Frosty.

"Swudge," the baby cooed, reaching for my bobbing antennae. "*Suuu*dge."

"Holy Toledo!" Pepper's mom looked stunned. "Did you hear that? I think Jo-No's saying her first word!"

The baby kept repeating the same mystery word and all attention was on her bubbly mouth. I kinda could care less, but folded an ear out from my headgear to pretend to hear better.

"Fudge? Such?" Pepper's mom guessed, smoothing down a dollop of Jo-No's red fuzz. "Lunch? Is that what you're saying, angel? Lunch?"

"It's really weird, you guys," I said, "it almost sounds like she's saying – sludge?"

"Bingo!" Pepper's mom was elated. "Wait . . ." Then deflated. "What the heck kind of a word is that?"

Pepper reached over and pulled her mom's coat open. "Hello? It's only plastered across your bazooms."

"Cripes!" I screeched. I couldn't believe she was wearing a

bright yellow T-shirt with SLUDGE printed on it. Sludge-mania was running amok! "Where'd you get that?"

"This?" she muttered, looking down at her chest. "I forgot I even had it on. Some of the Fireballs were going door-to-door last night with a petition, giving them away – for the price of a signature."

"Was one of them freakishly tall with a buzz cut?" I asked. "And horns?"

"Tell him what the petition was *for*, Ma."

"Oh, something to do with phys-ed funding. Things have gotten so bad, apparently, their coach just got the boot."

"That's bogus," I snapped.

"You left out the part about them wanting to can the Arts Committee," Pepper added. "And stopping the production of *Oliver!* I can't believe you signed that thing."

"Why not? Pepper, you love sports. Don't act like you don't all of a sudden."

"What? This is freakin' unbelievable!" I roared. "The jocks have had the spotlight on them since – forever. Now that the school is finally throwing us creative types a crumb, they're acting like big babies. No offense, Joy-Noelle."

"Sludge!" she spouted.

"They won't let up until all the drama geeks are wiped off the planet!"

"Oh, Dustin, don't be so dramatic," Pepper's mom said, lowering Jo-No back into her stroller.

"With all due respect, ma'am, please take off your shirt."

She snorted. "What am I supposed to do? Run around the mall in my brassiere?"

"It wouldn't be the first time," Pepper said. She got a smack on the butt for that one. "Kidding, Mother!"

"Boy, you've got some mouth on you." Pepper's mom snatched the ducky pacifier that Jo-No had tossed onto the ground and pocketed it. "I know I'll never be able to drag you away from Dustin," she said, buckling the baby into her stroller, "so meet us in front of Cinnabuns in an hour. C'mon, Joy-Joy, let's go spend your father's money."

My face was on fire as I watched Pepper's mom push her sister's stroller into the Casual Corner. "I can't believe that Zack is taking this thing so far. His drill-sergeant father is probably behind the whole thing – how much you wanna bet?" I tugged on the collar of my costume, pumping it for air. "Jeez, I'm sweatin' bullets in this thing. Talk about chestnuts roasting on an open fire."

Pepper picked up a stack of fliers and fanned me with it. "You got yourself all worked up, didn't ya? I like a man with convictions."

"Is that what I am?"

"That's what 'you am.'" She handed me the stack and without warning, took off toward the escalators shouting, "Back in a sec!"

I tried to calm myself down so I could get back to the job

at hand. "Smashum Brothers Pest Control. Twenty bucks off." Hardly any takers. You'd think I was charging for the darn things. "Get rid of your filthy vermin just in time for the holidays!"

"I'll have one of those."

Speaking of vermin, it was Candy Garboni. I almost fell back into the potted palms. She was wearing a lime green leopard-print jacket – over her SLUDGE shirt, of course, and a short jeans skirt. I didn't want her to recognize me, so I turned my face quickly toward the pillar.

"Hi, Dustin!"

The *mirrored* pillar.

"Don't try to hide – I can see your reflection. You look so cute. What're you supposed to be, like, a Christmas moth?"

"Yes. The traditional Christmas moth."

She stuck her face in mine and rolled her eyeballs around. "My dad finally sprung for contacts. You like?"

"Just keep moving along, miss," I said in my iciest voice. "You're holding up traffic."

"Du-*ust*," she whined, with a hip jut and a hair flip. "You don't hate me, do you?"

"Get rid of your obnoxious two-faced pests! Kill them dead!"

"C'mon, don't!" I wouldn't look directly at her, but I think there was bouncing up and down. "I hate it when people hate me. Can't we still be friends?" Yes, there was definite bouncing. And then came the bug-hug.

See, here's the thing. Even though Candy was a two-faced snitch, I couldn't stop myself from overheating when she wrapped her arms around my thorax. She smelled like fresh strawberries and vanilla – like one of those fancy, expensive candles. So the fact that she was clinging on a little too long wasn't the worst thing in the world.

"*Ooh!* Shoot. I can't believe it!" she cried. "I think my new charm bracelet is caught – on your thingamajig. And Zack gave it to me!"

"What gumball machine did he get *that* from?" I said, checking it out. No response. "Don't come cryin' to me when your wrist turns green and your hand falls off."

"That was just mean."

"Are you gonna run home now and tell him I said that?"

"No," she answered with a fierce tug. "Don't have to. He's right downstairs outside the Sports Shack – getting signatures on his petition to stop your precious show."

"Oh, perfect."

A clump of Candy's long hair was now stuck to the Velcro on the back of my costume. And the more she maneuvered to free herself, the more she got tangled in wings and things. People must've thought we were, like, a living sculpture of bug parts, legs and hair. Finally, Pepper came huffing and puffing to our rescue and with a single *rip!* we were free. Candy took off immediately without so much as a "see ya later."

"Uh, you're welcome," Pepper called out after her. "It's

autumn, in case you haven't noticed – buy a freakin' pair of pants!" We both watched as Candy disappeared around the enormous snowman, tugging at her skirt. "Here, dude, I got you a Dr Pepper, my signature drink." She held the straw from the giant plastic container to my lips and I took a slurpy sip. "Seriously, who dresses like that in this weather? And what's with all the makeup? She's obviously covering up a fresh crop of prepubescent zits."

"I dunno, she still looks pretty hot in makeup. You've gotta give her that."

"Get real!" Pepper yelled, shoving me. Hard. "You serious?"

"Sure, why not?" I steadied myself and set the soda down on the rim of a giant planter. "Listen, I really should get back to work. I've got this whole box of fliers left."

Pepper took her sweet time bending my crooked wings back into place before heading toward Bergmann's. The next half hour dragged by as I handed out five fliers at a time to whoever would take them, and most wound up in the trash can by Borders Books. This job really bit. My costume was starting to smell like the inside of a bowling shoe – and people didn't even know what I was supposed to be. So far I'd been mistaken for a butterfly, a moth, a bee, a wasp, Lord of the Flies, and the Sugarplum Fairy.

"Here. Take. Save." I bent over to grab my final handful and saw Wally and his bassoon approaching. *Friends are com-*

ing outta the woodwork! And that wasn't just the termite in me talking.

"Hey, Wally! It's me – Dustin. What the heck are you doing here?"

"Opus Five is performing," he said with a steely tone. "It's our first real gig."

No wisecracks about me being dressed up in a bug suit – with wings?

"Wow," I gushed. "That's huge! Why didn't you tell me?"

"I tried."

"You did? I don't remember."

Members of his quintet paraded by dressed in matching black pants and white shirts with shiny red ties, carrying their instruments. The Oxymoron gave me a quick smirk.

"Whatever," Wally grumbled. "Gotta go." And he rushed to catch up with the others.

Out of habit I almost hollered, "Call me later!" but the words got stuck in my better judgment. I knew at that exact moment that we weren't best friends anymore – that we hadn't been in a while. Artistic differences? Could be. I guess it was time to face the music. But when the strains of "God Rest Ye Merry Gentlemen" started flowing out of Opus Five, I just wanted to escape. Little by little SLUDGE-wearing passersby appeared, making things worse. *Can this day get any weirder?*

"Mirror, mirror on the wall, who's the fairest of the mall?"

Yes, it can. It was Pepper, dripping in goopy glamour makeup, primping in the mirrored pillar next to me. *Maybe there was something in the Hinkleyville water.*

"Fairest of the *mall*?" she repeated, batting her eyelashes so fast she was about to take flight. "Get it?"

"You're a regular riot. But what the heck happened to your face?"

"I've been glamourized. So whaddya think?" she asked with a lick of her varnished lips. "Am I – hot?"

"C'mon, Pep, quit goofin' around."

"What makes you think I'm goofin' around? What if I'm serious?" She moved closer and closer until I was pinned up against the pillar. I swear, she was ogling me like Wally does bacon-double-cheeseburgers. "I wanna know for real. Do you, Dustin Grubbs, think I'm hot? Yes or no? Honest answer."

"Umm . . . uhhh . . ." I could feel it in the pit of my stomach – this was no joke! Pepper closed her eyes, like she was coming in for a smooch. Freak-out time! I took a gigantic step backward and – *"Argh!"* – stumbled into a dense forest of potted palms.

"Are you all right?"

I was frantically trying to untangle myself and find my balance, fighting through rigid stalks and pointy palm fronds. Finally I managed to rip my way free, scrambling out the other side. And wouldn't you know it? Zack was standing right there, fuming – practically foaming at the mouth. I attempted to ignore him as I straightened out my scrunched-up antennae – until I realized he was aiming something right at me. Red. Shiny. *Lethal?* It looked exactly like a supersize can of Extra Strength

"Raid!"

Chapter 18

An Oliver *Twist!*

If I hadn't shielded my face in time, I might've ended up looking like the Phantom of the Opera. The last I saw of Zack he
was escaping through a Baby Gap with Pepper chasing after
him. I hope he ends up in mall-jail. It almost all seemed worth
it, though, when I was paid my seventy-five dollars salary in
cash! Unfortunately, it was gone before I hit the exit. There
was this "Give Peas a Chance" sweatshirt I had to have. Oh,
and I bought a real neat wedding present for Aunt Olive: a
silver dragonfly pin with blue crystal stones. The saleslady
said it was crafted in the style of some dead Russian named
Faberge, and that I had "exquisite taste."

Mr. Smashum dropped me off and I jetted up to my room
to avoid the "so how did things go?" question. There was a
note taped to my door. McKenna Casting, Inc. had called! My
last-ditch effort with Ballads-to-Go had paid off! *I knew it
was genius!* An earlier time slot had become available – 12:55,

and I was supposed to call them back ASAP to confirm or cancel. I was psyched at first, but then I realized – *Switching my callback from 1:40 to 12:55 isn't gonna help. The wedding is at two!* I wanted to self-destruct.

"Mom!" I called out into the hall. "Hey, M*ooo*m!" No answer.

Still loopy from bug spray, I threw myself across my bed, crumpling the note into a hard wad. Things were back to square one. Indecision throbbed inside me as I watched the falling leaves skittering past my window – dried up and dead, like so many missed opportunities. I thought about fall turning into winter and Aunt Olive turning into Mrs. Smashum. I thought about Wally's friendship turning sour – and Pepper's turning just plain weird. I wondered how many more people would blow out of my life before I even made it to high school.

"Knock, knock. So how did things go?"

It was Aunt Olive standing in my doorway, munching on a celery stick. I grabbed the dragonfly-pin box that was sitting on my bed and slipped it under my pillow.

"Great. I had a blast."

"I knew you would. Listen, I just had a crazy thought. Kind of a favor, actually. You don't have to say yes, but I have to ask."

Now what? Selling used cars in a bumblebee costume?

"It dawned on me this morning that I didn't have anyone to walk me down the aisle. Granny's certainly not going to do it – she may not even show up at all. I thought of Gordy, but – I know that's not exactly his cup of tea. So, whaddya say? Are you up for the task?"

Well, there it was. Smack-dab in front of me. The moment of truth.

"I – I –"

"You don't have to give me your answer right now."

"I think that'd be awesome."

She tried not to let me see the tear zigzagging down her cheek – and I tried not to let her see mine. My aunt crunched her way out into the hall and pulled the door shut behind her. That's when my water main broke. I must've sobbed quietly for a solid hour, practically drowning Cinnamon, who was snuggled up under my chin. The next thing I remembered was someone snapping one of those Hollywood clapboard things in my face and shouting, "Action!" Suddenly I was lying in a termite-filled bathtub wearing nothing but my coconut swim trunks and a furry Russian Cossack hat. When the ringing phone woke me up, I was gritting my teeth with the cat curled up on my head.

"Siberia Hilton," I murmured into the receiver.

"Dusty?"

"Dad?"

He was calling to let me know that his agent had called McKenna Casting on my behalf, but there wasn't a thing she could do. I told him it was officially over; that I was throwing in the towel and canceling my callback. I kind of got sloppy in the middle of it and fell apart all over again. Couldn't help it. Dad seemed to take it even harder than me.

"Man, oh, man, I'm so sorry, kid! Are you sure something can't be worked out?"

"I tried. Believe me. Ain't gonna happen."

"Wow. I know how disappointed you must be. But you'll have plenty more opportunities, no doubt about that. At least you've got your school musical to look forward to, right? Still – Jeez, Louise, I wish there was something I could do to make you feel . . ."

Long pause. Cinnamon was vibrating the whole bed as I stroked her head. A pity purr. I guess she wasn't so bad for a cat.

"I'm still here. Let me run something by you. How do you think your aunt Olive would react if I showed up next Saturday – to her wedding?"

"Are you kidding?" I sat upright. "Omigod, it'd make her day! It'd make everyone's day. Almost."

"Oh, don't worry about your grandma. Her bark is worse than her bite."

"Especially when she's not wearing her false teeth."

"It's about time I showed my face – cleared the air," Dad said in a serious voice, not even noticing my joke. "But keep it under your hat, okay? 'Cause I want it to be a surprise."

*　　　*　　　*

I think I slept through most of Sunday. Come Monday morning, I headed for BMF Elementary an hour early, bruised but hopeful. The *Oliver!* cast list was supposed to be posted first thing, and I wanted to beat the crowds. It wasn't the big-time, but at least it was something. Call me crazy, but I told myself that if I could make it all the way to school without stepping on a single sidewalk crack, my name would be listed after "Artful Dodger" – even after my rocky audition. I mean if my commercial thing hadn't fallen through, Dad never would be coming to the wedding, right? So good things can come from bad – and miracles can happen when you least expect them.

I clung to that thought as I ambled down Main Street. It was still semidark out so I couldn't help noticing the light come on in Miss Pritchard's Academy of Dance. The tops of Dad's tap shoes were visible – sitting on the windowsill where I'd left them, like loaves of patent-leather bread. With no classes going on yet, I figured it was the perfect time to run up and get them. So I flew up the skinny stairway and through the reception area. When I pressed my nose onto the window of the dance studio door, I thought my eyeballs were playing tricks on me.

"Check. It. Out," I mumbled to myself.

It was Zack. Kincaid! Even though I only saw him from behind, I'd know that blond bonehead anywhere. He had a leg stretched over the bar like a ballerina and Miss Pritchard was coaching him. "Flat back," I heard her say. "Point your toes. Nice, easy stretch." The room was empty except for the two of them. Talk about surreal. "Good. Now assume first position, and we'll move onto *demi pliés*."

Zack spun around. I quickly ducked down, whacking a knee into the door.

"Cripes!"

"Is somebody there?" Miss Pritchard called out. "Can I help you?"

In a crouched position I scurried toward the exit as quietly as possible, and flew down the stairs. Clomping footsteps were right behind me. Just as I was about to grab the outside doorknob I was yanked from behind and thrown into the banister.

"Oow! My el-bone!"

"You ain't going nowhere, dude!"

"It was a free country last time I looked. Whaddya gonna do to me this time, Zack – flush me down the toilet?"

"Boys?" Miss Pritchard barked from the top landing. "What's going on?"

"Nothin'. We're cool," Zack told her. "Just gimme five minutes." She lingered a little before disappearing and Zack turned his attention back to me. "You gotta hear me out, okay?"

I looked up at him in his crusty ballet slippers, breathing

heavily like an obscene phone caller. I definitely had the upper hand – why was I running off? "All right, you twisted my arm." *Literally.* "So talk."

"I'm prob'ly just wastin' my breath tellin' you this, but . . . I wanna be a professional basketball player someday. Not wanna be – *gonna* be. And I'll do whatever it takes." His face was blotchy red except for his left eye, which was purple and swollen. He'd probably leaped when he should've twirled. "But my knees are kinda messed up, see. So my dad has me come here 'cause the exercises help increase my flexibility – to prevent injuries, improve my jumps. Lots of pros do it." Suddenly he pounded the wall with his fist. "Ah, you don't understand!"

"I'm not as dumb as you look. So what's the problem?"

Zack stared at the ground and took to knuckle-cracking. "If the guys found out about this ballet thing, the other Fireballs – I'd be dead meat for sure, I mean they'd really lay into me." Then he looked me right in the face. "So what's it gonna take, man – to shut you up? Make me an offer."

"For real?"

Hmm, I'm glad I stuck around. I was going through a list of demands in my head – destroy all SLUDGE shirts; destroy petition to ban the Arts Committee and stop our musical; slip a thousand dollars in unmarked bills into my locker by noon tomorrow – when all of a sudden Zack started wheezing. Bad. Before I could get "You okay?" out of my mouth, he was bent over, clutching his chest, and gasping for air like a drowning man.

"Miss Pritchard!" I yelled. "Come quick!"

By the time she got to him, Zack was already taking hits off an asthma inhaler he'd dug out of his sweatpants. Miss Pritchard mumbled something about the dusty hall, and how this happened from time to time, and assured me he'd be fine. She helped Zack up the stairs and I exited onto the street, amazed at the scene that had just played out.

I was on a power trip as I power-walked the rest of the way to school. Catching ballerina-Zack was like a Get-Out-of-Jail-Free card – I could whip it out and use it the next time he bared his fangs. But the more I thought about it, the more I actually started admiring the jerk in spite of myself. *Asthma and weak knees – yet still determined to be a professional basketball player. Talk about beating the odds.* As soon as I'd set foot through the school doors, it hit me: I'd forgotten the stupid tap shoes again!

"Congratulations, Dustin!" Stewy called out, then sputtered down the hall like a deflating balloon, shouting, "I can't believe it, I can't believe it!" I made a beeline to the bulletin board outside the main office. There was a gaggle of girls stuck to it like paper clips to a magnet – the cast list had been posted for sure. I craned my neck to see through all the bouncing heads. The first name I spotted was

Oliver Twist: S. Ziggler

Stewy? That little Dickens! Couldn't have happened to a nicer kid, but where the heck's my name? I weaved my way to the front of the clump. Most of the adult parts had been given to high-schoolers, and there were pages and pages of orphans and pickpockets thanks to that no-cuts policy – just like with the Fireballs. I hunted for "Grubbs," and landed on

Artful Dodger: D. Deluca

Say it isn't so! They gave my part to a girl? No, that rare sub-species of girl known as Darlene Deluca. No fair – since when are girls allowed to play boys? It's not like we're doing Peter Pan! I took a second to get a grip. *Okay, it's not the end of the world. There are still a bunch of juicy roles left.*

My eyes shot up and down the page as if I were speed-reading in Japanese. Mr. Bumble . . . Mr. Sowerberry . . . Dr. Grimwig – not me, not me, not me.

Finally, there it was: "Grubbs!" *Hallelujah.* After the role of Bill Sikes. "Yes!" I shouted, hugging the third-grader next to me. They'd actually given me one of the adult parts! But then I thought, *Wait – Bill Sikes? The villain? That bear of a man who kicks his dog and beats Nancy to death at the end? That's quite a stretch even for me. But I guess with some fake beard stubble and shoulder pads I could pass as a psychopathic brute. This will be my greatest acting challenge yet!*

The instructions said to initial the cast list to indicate that we'd accepted our parts. I was eagerly plucking a pen from my backpack, when a bloodcurdling scream came from behind. It was Darlene. "I'm guessing that was a scream of joy?" I asked as she butted her way next to me.

"Omigawd, are you kidding? I got the best role in the whole show. Two great numbers in act one – what's not to like? I didn't know they were allowed to cast girls as boys."

"Me neither."

"Gimme your pen." She swiped it out of my hand and initialed the list so enthusiastically she tore through the paper. I swiped it back and was about to put my DG after the role of Bill Sikes when Darlene yanked my arm down.

"What're ya doin', dork? Your name's down there. See?"

Megamouth was right. There it was – near the bottom.

Noah Claypole: D. Grubbs

"*Noah Claypole?*" I muttered. "I'm not even sure who that – *Ugh!* The pimply undertaker's assistant? But he's only in one short scene!"

"And it's a nonsinging, nondancing role," Darlene happily reminded me. "Guess you can't be the star of every show, huh?" I had a strong urge to tap-dance on her smugly face. But before I could even say anything, she turned her nose up and went skipping down the hall, rubbing it in with "Not everyone can be a triple threat!"

Oh, the inhumanity! That meant I was practically in the chorus. One step away from being a freakin' tree. My eyes zoomed back up the list. It really did say G. Grubbs after Bill Sikes – not D. Grubbs. *G as in Gordy? As in my brother? Nuh-uh.*

No way. There had to be another G. Grubbs at Fenton High. Either that or demons are skating around in Hades catching snowflakes on their forked tongues 'cause it has definitely frozen over!

"Hey, you," I heard in my ear. Pepper had snuck up on me – smelling like a girly-girl.

Riiing! Saved by the bell! Without a word, I took off sprinting down the hall.

"What's the rush?" she called out after me. I switched into second gear, passing Stewy, who was still whirling with joy. "Don't you wanna find out what happened to Zack at the mall? Let's just say my kickboxing lessons really came in handy!"

"What?" I skidded to a halt and did an about-face. "Is that how he got that shiner? I don't need you or anybody else to do my fighting for me."

"I was just trying to –"

"I think I know what you were trying to do," I shot back. "Listen, I'm gonna need you to – just back off a little. Okay?"

And friendship number two bites the dust. My life, like Stewy Ziggler, was spinning out of control. I galloped to the end of the hall where Miss Van Rye was herding her bubbly brood of kindergartners into her classroom.

"Excuse me," I called out, catching her by surprise. "But we need to talk."

"Oh, Dustin, can it wait? Let me get my kiddlings settled in first, and then –"

"I just wanna know if the G. Grubbs on the cast list is my brother?"

"Oh, he's perfect for the role of Bill Sikes, don't you think? He has a natural gruffness about him and a strong presence. And such a nice, loud singing voice. Talent certainly runs in your family."

Brain overload! Cannot compute!

Then it hit me like a ton of bricks and suddenly it all made sense. My acting book showing up in Gordy's room; over-hearing his phone conversation about singing that Foo Fighters song; fisticuffs! *He wants fisticuffs? I'll give him fisticuffs!*

"Well, I'm glad you're so in love with him – but you can count me out." I took in a lungful of the Play-Doh and paste smell wafting out of the kindergarten room. "I've been told by real professionals that charm and charisma are just puls-ing through my veins – that I'm something special. I'm not playing no Noah stinkin' Claypole!"

"Oh, hon, you *are* special. But Noah has that riveting scene where he picks a fight with Oliver – you'll be fabulous! And you know what they say, 'There are no small parts, only small –'"

"Actors, I know. But that's just a bogus saying, like, 'It doesn't matter if you win or lose, it's how you play the game.' The truth is, there *are* small parts and winning *does* matter! So you can count me out – I'm not doing the show!"

"B.J., don't!" Miss Van Rye yelled, poking her head into her classroom. "Stop jostling Jocelyn!"

"This was all Mr. Lynch's idea, wasn't it? He hates my guts."

"Oh, on the contrary –"

The second bell rang. I started to leave, but she grabbed my arm. "Dustin, I really wish you'd reconsider."

"Well – some wishes don't come true."

Chapter 19

Disappearing Act

I was beaten down. Hollow. Kicked in the shins by the show-biz gods and considering a new career in – I don't know, patio furniture sales? I had refused to speak to Gordy all week – just totally steered clear. But Friday after school, I was forced to share a Hyundai with him and Mom.

See, Granny had insisted that their "bug problem" was getting worse, and she didn't want the wedding guests thinking we lived like a bunch of hillbillies. So Mr. Smashum offered to fumigate the entire downstairs the night before the wedding. No charge. Major suck-up. Mom told Granny and my aunts they could all spend the night in our apartment and we would just stay over at the Dew Drop Inn, since we were picking up Aunt Olive's dress near there anyway. But really we were picking up Dad too. The plan was to sneak him home the next day so he could pop out of the wedding cake and surprise Aunt Olive. Not really pop out of the cake but same basic concept. Dad's idea was brilliant – the only glimmer of light in my otherwise rock-bottom existence. As long as he didn't bail.

"Gawd, Mom," I whined from the backseat. "Aren't we there yet?"

"You're driving like an old lady," Gordy said. "Why won't you let me get behind the wheel?"

"Because I want to get there in one piece. Can't you guys find something constructive to do? I can remember when you'd both be entertained for hours with just a coloring book and a box of crayons."

"That was, like, a hundred years ago," I reminded her. "One of us has matured since then. I'm not mentioning any names."

I'd only brought along my history textbook, *Conflict of a Nation.* The thing is, it was the sort of book that once you put it down, you just couldn't pick it up. I cracked it open anyway. The unread postcard I was using as a bookmark slipped out.

Hi, DG,
Major disaster! My dad's decided to stay out here for another 3 months. At least! He loves it. Mom hates it. I'm freaking out somewhere in the middle.

XO
Ellen

P.S. - Be home soon, I guess. Kiss the kitty.

Hmm, it looks like LMNOP and I finally have something in common – nomad dads. Just then Gordy whipped out his *Oliver!* script and started highlighting his lines – obviously to torture me. Even though the marker fumes filled the car, I decided to ignore him. Be the better man. So I stared out the window thinking positive thoughts; reveling in the amazing Crayola colors of the beautiful autumn day. The Mango Tango leaves blanketing the hillsides; the Radical Red maple trees blazing in the sun; the Laser Lemon marker *sweeping* across the pages of my hateful brother's script!

"Mom," I yelled, "tell him to stop!"

"Stop what? I didn't even do anything."

"Dustin, he didn't even do anything," Mom echoed.

"He stole my life!"

And the gloves were officially off.

"Up yours, dweeb!" Gordy jabbed, glaring over the seat-back. "I just got two words for you: Jea-lous."

"Don't start!" Mom clicked on the radio. "This is supposed to be a happy occasion, so can we please just have a little happy? One more outburst and I'm switching to the country station."

She wasn't kidding either. Eventually the *swish* of the marker turned into the *swish* of branches brushing against the car as we pulled up in front of the motel. I could see the blue LuvQUEST.com sign of Dad's cab sticking up in the parking lot. Things were looking up – he'd actually showed!

"Hello, gorgeous family!" Dad greeted us from the doorway of the motel room, balancing an ice bucket on his head. "Perfect timing – I just got here myself. I'm in the adjoining single, but I stocked your minifridge with Cokes in case you're thirsty."

I attacked Dad with a fierce hug, and Gordy gave him a quick one on his way to the soda stash. Mom was following it up with a peck on the cheek when it hit me: The four of us were altogether in the same room for the first time since – forever. My career may have been taking a nosedive but there was major progress on the home front. No wonder Dad seemed wired for sound.

"Hey, Gord! Man, you're looking buff. You been working out? Lemme see those guns." *Oh, puke.* "So what's all this about you getting a part in the musical? I was floored when your mother told me – thought she was pullin' my leg."

I took a deep breath of pine and mildew and belly flopped onto one of the beds, determined to keep my cool. It turns out The Dew Drop Inn was the perfect name for the joint because everything was damp – even the covers.

"Everybody knew Dustin had greasepaint in his blood," Dad went on, "but, when'd *you* get bitten by the acting bug?"

"When he stole my life!" So much for keeping my cool.

"Shaddup, Freakshow!"

"Not a good topic of conversation, Ted," Mom said from the other end of the room. She was taking clothes out of her suitcase and hanging them on hangers, even though we were only staying for one damp night.

"It started as a joke – Rebecca dared me to try out 'cause I needed extracurricular activities on my college aps. Who knew they'd cast me in the stupid thing?" I buried my head under two pillows, but I could still hear. ". . . my English-lit teacher said he'd guarantee me at least a C-plus if I went through with it. I know it's lame, but I guess it ain't gonna kill me, right?"

That still didn't explain why he kept the whole thing a big secret from me.

"Listen, boys, I have to go pick up your aunt's dress," Mom said as I emerged from the pillows. "And before I go, your father and I have to talk."

"So talk," Gordy grunted.

"We need some alone time. Why don't you watch TV in the next room or check out the pool or something so we can have a little privacy."

"But it's an outdoor pool," Gordy complained. "And it's October. It's probably empty."

"So's your head," I told him. "Do you need a brick to fall on you? C'mon."

Gordy followed me out the door and I swear he checked out the ceiling for falling bricks. He immediately took off without me, sloshing through wet fallen leaves along the stretch of the motel.

"Hey, turdface, wait up!" I called out, but he kept going.

"Eat dirt and die."

Nothing like brotherly love to warm the cockles of your heart. I caught up with him at the back of the hotel next to a trickling creek. Gordy sat up on the warped picnic table, gnawing on dead thumbnail skin.

"Okay, I think we should call a truce," I said, straddling the bench. Water droplets were falling from a giant elm, dotting the table and sending shivers down my back. "You know, a cease-fire, a peace agreement – make nice." I wanted to get the meaning across in case *truce* wasn't part of his third-grade vocabulary. "Just till after the wedding, while Dad's around. I don't know if he ever mentioned it to you, but when I was in Chicago he told me he was thinking of moving back to Buttermilk Falls. Maybe. And who knows? Mom and Dad might even be able to finally work things out."

"You're dreamin'."

"Seriously! That's probably what they're talking about right now. Lots of people get remarried to the same people they'd divorced. Mr. Futterman did."

"Yeah. After his ex-wife went and got her bumpers overhauled at her plastic surgeon's."

"Hey, a recon-silicone-iation! Bah-*dum*-pum!"

That gem deserved a standing ovation, but Gordy barely cracked a smile.

"Well, whatever," I said in my back-to-business voice, "No more fighting or we might drive him away for good. Deal?"

Gordy let out the longest, loudest belch I'd ever heard in my life. I mean, they could hear it in New Jersey. Then he ripped off a strip of dead fingernail skin with his teeth and spit it into a bush before finally nodding in agreement.

"Should we shake on it," I asked, "to seal the deal?"

"I ain't shakin' nothin'."

That was the best I was going to get out of him. I left Gordy to his shredded fingers and gas, and headed back to our "suite." The lamp was on in our room, and I could see Mom and Dad sitting at the table near the window gazing at each other. *Longingly?* My conversation with Gordy was still fresh in my mind, so I wasn't sure if what I was seeing was for real or just wishful thinking. I hid behind a pungent and pinchy, wet pine tree to watch – okay, spy.

Nothing but a lot of gabbing going on and I was sinking into the mud, so I'd almost reconsidered – until Dad reached across the table and took Mom's hand – no, wait – *both* hands into his and wasn't letting go. *Interesting. But too good to be true?* There was more talking; some nodding. Laughter – always a good sign. Then Mom rose from her chair and floated over to Dad's side of the table. *And the plot thickens.* Hard to see with the darn curtains in the way, but it looked like she was touching his shoulders. *Okay, that's more like it.* Make that *massaging* his shoulders. *Whoa!* And she didn't let up for quite a while. (I tried high-fiving the squirrel next to me, but he scrambled up the tree.) Suddenly I heard a scuffing noise coming from the room and when I looked back in, Dad was on his feet – *shoot* – and the chair was between the two of them. *No, don't walk away! Stay . . . stay. . . .* And as if he could hear my thoughts, he inched around the chair getting closer to Mom. Closer – even closer. . . . *And, ladies and gentlemen, they said it'd never happen, but there you have it – a full frontal embrace!*

Just then Gordy trudged up to the doorstop, scraping muddy leaves off his shoes. Spell broken.

"Don't go in!" I whispered, rushing over to him. "I think they're having – a moment."

"Tough. I gotta take a leak."

Mom and Dad pulled away from each other when the moment-killer barged into the room. And right after that Mom left to go pick up Aunt Olive's wedding dress while Dad took a nap. Amazingly, Gordy and I stuck to our truce, even while no one was watching. I'm guessing he was just as gung ho as

I was for the parental units to get together, but too cool to admit it. When it came time for lights-out, Mom insisted that the scum-bucket and I sleep in the same bed. I should've seen it coming – there were only two double-beds in the room and she'd refused to pay extra for a cot.

"Mom, don't do this to me," I begged. "I won't even share the same stage with Gory – I mean Gordy, so how can I share the same bed? Things would work out perfectly if you'd just sleep in the next room with Dad."

"I'm going to pretend I didn't hear that," she said, switching off the lamp. "Now get some sleep. We've got a big day ahead of us."

Gordy immediately claimed the good side of the bed, without the cigarette burns or questionable stains. I formed a dividing wall between us with extra pillows. A second later, they were on the floor. Two seconds later, I was on the floor. After a game of "blanket tug-of-war" and "dodge the three-inch toenails," Gordy finally fell asleep. I was left scrunched up on a small triangle of bed, steaming mad and very awake. I knew I'd be stuck in that position all night, waiting for the sunrise – so I rolled out of bed, tiptoed to Dad's door, and knocked lightly.

It squeaked open and I slipped into his room, which apparently came with a fog machine. *Again with the secondhand cigarette smoke? It's a wonder I'm not already hooked up to an iron lung.*

"Can't you sleep?" Dad whispered. "Lumpy mattress?"

"Lumpy brother."

"Well, you're welcome to crash in here if you want."

It was dark except for the bluish flickering light of the TV, but I could still see stuff strewn everywhere. Dad sat on the edge of his bed and snuffed out his cigarette in the plastic ashtray on the nightstand. "Come on, hop in," he said, patting the mattress. "Let me just switch off the boob tube."

"You can keep it on. I'm not really that sleepy yet."

Dad peeled back the covers and we both climbed in between the cool, white sheets. And damp – did I mention damp? I couldn't decide if it was Dad or the bed that smelled like musty wool. It was strangely comforting, though. Like a broken-in easy chair.

"There ya go. Snug as a bug in a rug." He gave his pillow a good punch and propped it up against the headboard. "The weatherman said the temperature's gonna plunge into the thirties tonight. And tomorrow it may even snow."

"Oh, crud! Aunt Olive's planned a big outdoor wedding."

"Well, that should be interesting." Dad smirked, scratching his sandpapery neck. "I hope the groom doesn't get cold feet!"

"Bah-*dum*-pum!" we both said at the same time.

"*Ha!* Good one, Pops. You should write that down."

"Listen, kid, do me a favor and plug in my cell phone, will ya?" He was speed-flipping through the channels with the remote. "It's on the table next to you. I keep forgetting to recharge the doggone thing and I need to check my messages."

Scooching up on one elbow, I felt around the wrappers and empty cans on the nightstand until I found the electrical cord that went with the cell phone. Finally, I attached it, plugged it into the wall outlet, and collapsed onto my pillow with a noisy exhale.

"Freddy baby!" Dad cried out as an old black-and-white movie flashed on the TV screen. It was the one where Fred Astaire tap-dances on the walls and ceiling. *Royal Wedding.* How appropriate, right? I tell ya, they don't make 'em like that anymore."

"You know, I took a tap class once. With your old tap shoes."

"I had tap shoes?"

"Yeah. You don't even remember?" He jutted out his lip and rolled his eyes around. That was a no. "Found them in the attic. Anyway, it turned out to be a disaster."

"Two left feet?" he asked, yawning.

"Two left kayaks," I answered, yawning. "But I'm thinking of giving it another shot."

"You should." Dad melted into a fetal position with one leg over the covers, hugging his extra pillow. "Nobody becomes a Fred Astaire in one lesson, kid. It takes years of practice."

"Especially dancing on ceilings like that."

"You know what I mean."

Dad's eyelids were struggling to stay open. It struck me funny that he was conking out while Fred was bouncing off the walls and working up a sweat.

"It's not easy – showing your face again in a place where you really screwed up." Dad sounded soft and serious. "It takes a lot of guts. But you know what they say . . ."

I waited for the "no guts, no glory" capper. It never came. He was out like a light. Dad's face seemed gigantic to me – like it belonged on Mount Rushmore or something, and I couldn't help studying it up close. I wondered if I'd have the same salt-and-pepper beard stubble someday; wondered if weird thickets of hair would decide to grow out of my ears too. *I could definitely live without that.* Except for the Big Dipper mole formation on his forehead, the creases, and the receding hairline, it was like looking into a mirror. Well, a funhouse mirror.

"G'night, big guy," I whispered, clicking off the TV. "Glad to have you back."

He rolled to the far side of the bed and started a snorefest. Mom used to say he was sawing logs – more like chainsawing his way through Yosemite National Park. I fell right off to sleep, though, with a warm feeling coating my stomach like a sip of hot chocolate.

Woke up with that same exact feeling too – until I realized that Dad and all his stuff had disappeared.

216

Chapter 20

The Roar of the Crowd

There was a note sitting in the pillow dent where Dad's head had been. It was scrawled on Dew Drop Inn stationery, barely legible. He must've written it in a hurry, in the dark.

Guys,
Got urgent message from agent. Great job offer –
a six-month gig in Florida! Last-minute replacement.
Must be there tomorrow or it's a bust. Off to Chicago
to pick up Shelly, etc. – a million things to do. Please
understand! Love to Olive.
Dad

It was like a sucker punch to the soul. I lay frozen staring at the note, feeling numb – except for the paper cut I'd gotten, which was stinging. Throbbing. Burning. I thought I'd hit rock bottom before, but somehow I'd slipped through the cracks onto a layer of broken glass and worm guts. The logical part of me was thinking, *Oh, well, that's Dad for you. What're ya gonna do?* Another part of me wanted to hunt him down and pummel him!

Mom didn't say a thing when I showed her the note, as if nothing Dad did could surprise her anymore. But I heard her swearing under her breath while she stuffed Aunt Olive's wedding dress into the trunk of the car. I thought we were going to drive all the way home in silence, but halfway there she asked, "Who's Shelly?"

"A purple mermaid dummy. Part of his new ventriloquist act."

No further explanation was needed.

"No one has to know about any of this, okay?" Mom asked it like a question, but it was clearly an order. "His showing up at the wedding was going to be a surprise anyway, so not a word. You hear me?" She shot a look to me in the backseat and I nodded. "You hear me?" she asked Gordy directly. He grunted and kept staring straight ahead. Whenever he was really upset he always turned to stone.

Mom switched on the country classics radio station to wallow in some "he done me wrong" songs. I almost asked her what the deal was with all the hand-holding and that hug that I'd spied through the motel window, but Tammy Wynette started belting out "D-I-V-O-R-C-E" and Mom ripped the knob right out of the dashboard. So I'd decided to keep my big mouth S-H-U-T.

Traffic was thick when we got back to Buttermilk Falls, practically coming to a standstill near Fenton High. People were flocking to the school like it was All-You-Can-Eat-Ribs-Night at the Hog & Heifer. "What's going on?" Mom snapped, looking around. She kept honking her horn, getting more aggravated by the minute. "If I don't get that dress to your aunt real soon she'll have a conniption." Finally we came to a complete stop. "Look," she said, rolling down her window, "isn't that Pepper?"

I called out to her, giving her the international sign-language shrug for "What's going on?" The next thing I knew Pepper was shoving herself into the backseat of our Hyundai. That image of her all puckered up, covered in mall makeup, flashed in my brain and I scooched to the opposite side of the car.

"Don't worry, you're not gonna catch anything," she said, half out of breath. "Anyway, you won't believe what's happening. Out-and-out war! The Arts Committee and the Fenton High drama club are super P-O'ed. Excuse my French, Mrs. Grubbs. They've accused the jocks of stealing their spotlight."

"Well, duh," I said. "That's nothing new."

"No, their *actual* spotlight – from the high school

auditorium. It happened last night. Nobody can figure out how they broke in, or how they managed to rip it off 'cause that thing weighs a ton. Now the whole town has gone bonkers! They called an emergency meeting."

"When?"

"Right now. C'mon!"

Pepper threw open the car door and pulled me onto Cubberly Street.

"Isn't your brother coming?" she asked, more to him than me. We gave it a three-count, but Gordy didn't budge. "Guess not."

"The wedding's at two, mister, so you'd better be home and in your suit no later than one o'clock," Mom warned through the window. "I've had enough trauma for one day."

War chants were spilling out of the Fenton High auditorium, and the inside looked like one of those wild political conventions you see on TV. Only instead of red, white, and blue bunting dressing the stage, there was a droopy backdrop of London Bridge. A podium stood center stage, and to the left of it, in a lineup of chairs, were Miss Van Rye, Miss Honeywell, Mr. Lynch, and some angry high school drama teachers. Miss Blodget and a bunch of gym-teacher types were assembled to the right. Even Deputy-Sheriff Lutz was there, standing next to the American flag, with a hand resting on his nightstick like he might have to use it.

"Hey-hey, *clap-clap*, ho-ho, *clap-clap*, the Arts Committee has got to go!" rang out from the right half of the auditorium – the SLUDGE-shirt-wearing half. "Ho-ho, *clap-clap*, hey-hey, *clap-clap*, the Arts Committee has got to stay!" echoed from the left, where Pepper and I sat. There were a gaggle of cheerleaders in the middle rows, neutral like Switzerland, cheering for who knows what?

"People, people!" Futterman bellowed, stepping up to the podium and waving his arms. "Settle down. The principal from Fenton isn't here yet, so it looks like I'm running the show. People, *please!*" The chanting petered out and the shouting died down to a dull rumble. "Apparently there's been some criminal behavior here at the high school – but I can only address the tensions going on at BMF Elementary that might've led up to it." He cleared his throat. "Now I realize a lot of you are upset about the phys ed cutbacks, which may or may not have resulted in the Slam-Dunk Tourney going to Claymore this year – not to mention Coach Mockler." A chorus of *boo* rose up from half the audience, but Futterman overpowered it with "Believe me, I feel your pain. As everyone knows, I'm one big athletic supporter!"

That got a huge laugh. Futterman was clueless.

"But why all this rage is being directed at the Arts Committee and our musical is beyond me," Miss Van Rye complained.

"Ah, shut your piehole, lady," some guy heckled. "Everything was just fine until you artsy-fartsy folk entered the picture. I say we cancel that expensive theatrical of yours and put the money back into the sports teams where it belongs!"

A roar of approval came from the ESPN zone.

"But what about culture?" a woman shouted from the front row of our section. I think it was Miss Pritchard. "What about artistic expression? Feeding your soul?"

"That's a load of horse manure. Just feed my belly and pass me the remote!"

While half the crowd was rolling in the aisles, Maggie's mother popped up from our section hoisting a large plastic container. "I brought homemade fudge!" she announced. "If anyone's interested."

"How thoughtful, Mrs. Wathom," Futterman said, motioning for her to sit. "All right, pipe down, people. Everyone's entitled to an opinion, but here's the bottom line: The *Oliver!* performances will go on as planned – with or without a spotlight. Case closed."

Jeers from the SLUDGE side. Cheers from the fudge side.

"That ain't gonna stop us from picketing outside the auditorium," a man in overalls growled, "banging pots, and causing a ruckus! It's our fifth amendment right."

"First amendment, Otis," the deputy said, clomping toward the podium. "Bang a pot and I'll have to slap the cuffs on you. I'm pretty sure a peaceful demonstration is allowed, though – I'd have to look it up." He stepped up to the microphone, edging out Futterman. "Uh, pertaining to the matter of the felony committed on the premises, alls I got to say is whoever ripped off that spotlight had best return it, or I'll hunt 'em down and throw their butts in jail. Thank you for your time."

Pepper and I looked up at the balcony all sectioned off with yellow DO NOT CROSS police tape. "You think it was Zack and his two stooges?" she asked.

"Who else? With the help of Zack's Neanderthal dad, I'll bet."

"You heard the man – jail!" Futterman warned, regaining his position at the mic.

"All right then, if anyone has any questions or comments they'd like to make, please raise your hand and we'll take you one at a time. Yes, Mr. Kincaid? Come up to the microphone so everyone can hear you."

As Zack's dad was steamrolling his way toward the stage, Pepper leaned in close to whisper something and I flinched. Knee-jerk reaction. Okay, maybe just a jerk reaction. Whatever she was going to say turned into, "Remember when I pretended to put the moves on you at the mall? You knew that was a joke, right?"

"Good one."

"I was just horsin' around."

"Yeah, I know" – *that you're lying through your teeth.*

Truth is, she probably still had a crush. *I can't believe I was so clueless.* Maybe it would fade away eventually like a summer tan. As long as our friendship stayed put – that's all that mattered.

"Can everybody hear meee*EEEEIIIKK*!" Feedback. Mr. Kincaid backed off the mic. "I'm just gonna cut to the chase," he said, holding up a bunch of rumpled papers. "What I got here is a petition signed by half the people in this town in favor of canning the Arts Committee *and* their show. For good. Like Emmett said, it wasn't until they came along with their crazy ideas that our athletes started getting the shaft."

"That's absurd!" Mr. Lynch snarled. Hot, angry murmurs came from the other teachers onstage. I could feel the heat that had been brewing inside me all morning bubbling up to a boil as well. Even though I had turned down the show, Mr. Kincaid's words really ticked me off.

"I mean where are the new uniforms these kids were promised?" he fumed on. "Where's the digital scoreboard? Where's the coach?" He was tapping his finger on the podium as he spoke, like a hostile orchestra conductor with his baton. "Some of these boys got real talent. And everyone knows darn well if they're gonna have half a shot at going pro, they've gotta start young. Our schools need *more* funding to support these gifted kids – not less!"

"But what about the *other* gifted kids?" I hollered, shooting out of my seat. "Like the drama geeks or the music nerds?" My feet were starting down the aisle – I don't know what had possessed me. "Or that strange boy who's always hiding out in stairwells making up haiku? I'm sure you remember them, sir. You used to steal their lunch money when you were little."

The audience cracked up, fueling me even faster toward the stage.

"Listen, smart-mouth, Buttermilk Falls has always been a sports town!" Mr. Kincaid's whole head turned bright red. Really lit up, like Rudolph-the-Red-Necked-Reindeer's nose. "If folks want that sissified stuff they should move to the city with the rest of the freaks. That's all I got to say." He pushed away from the podium and slapped his petition into Futterman's chest.

"Good afternoon," I said taking over the microphone. "Dustin Grubbs, arts advocate. Sissified stuff, Mr. Kincaid? Meaning, like – oh, I don't know, *ballet,* for instance? It's funny, 'cause I happened to stop by Miss Pritchard's School of Dance the other day and you'll never guess who I ran into –"

I caught a glimpse of Zack's purple face scowling up at me, surrounded by an arsenal of Fireballs. *Brace yourself, sucker. It's payback time.* I was a breath away from getting even with him for all the shoves, the T-shirts – the Raid. But as I watched his gorilla of a dad barreling toward him, something clicked in my brain. Suddenly I saw Zack as just a gung ho kid with an impossible dream and a messed-up father. Suddenly he was me.

"Uh, never mind," I muttered, and left it at that. I could actually hear Zack's sigh of relief. "Anyway, here's how I see the situation. Some kids are great at shooting baskets, right? Like Zack Kincaid. And other kids are great at – maybe *weaving* baskets." The crowd groaned. "Some kids can wow a crowd with a triple play; other kids can wow a crowd with triple pirouettes and *acting* in a play." *Ugh.* "Well, you get my drift."

"Yeah, but what're you getting so high and mighty about, Benedict Arnold?" Darlene yelled from the second row. "You quit our play!"

"Excellent point." I wanted to wring her chicken neck. "Well, maybe I made a big mistake. It happens. Maybe I'm back in again – if it's not too late."

I turned to the Arts Committee to see Miss Honeywell and Miss Van Rye smiling big and nodding. Mr. Lynch actually gave me the thumbs-up! *Our Mr. Lynch?* There was a smattering of applause and a flashbulb went off. *Paparazzi?* This was getting cooler by the second. I was back at the mic, about to wrap things up when I felt a tugging at my rear end – and a draft. The next thing I know, London Bridge wasn't the only thing falling down! I bent over to hike up my sweatpants, then – *boom* – cut to me flailing on the ground drowning in slobber!

"No, baby, no!" I heard over running footsteps.

"I begged you not to, Vicky, but you did it anyway," Futterman groused as I struggled to my knees, wiping drool from my eyes. "You took him to the Pampered Pooch, didn't you?"

It was Shatzi! I should've recognized him by his pungent breath, if nothing else. He was sporting a new French poodle, pom-pom, show-dog cut – topped off with his fierce Doberman head. You didn't know whether he was going to dance the cancan or rip your face off.

"Shatzi, how ya doin', boy?" I gushed, scratching behind his pointed ears. "Did that nice vet in Normal make your leg all better?" It was wrapped in an embarrassingly pink bandage that matched his embarrassingly pink rhinestone collar. *Have mercy.*

"Wait a second – that was you?" the woman asked excitedly. She turned out to be the new and improved Mrs. Futterman, all platinum blond and inflated. "You're Dustin Grubbs, right? *You* rescued my baby?"

"Yeah, with my – my dad." Weird how I almost couldn't get the D-word out. "Didn't the vet tell you?" I said, rolling to my feet. "We left all our info with him – at least I think we did. We were in such a hurry that night – gawd, who knows?"

Mrs. Futterman took to rummaging through her purse while Shatzi took to humping my leg. With gusto. The audience was grumbling impatiently and I was struggling to save my dignity when Mrs. Futterman handed me a piece of a paper. A check – made out in my name. For "A thousand dollars?"

"Didn't you see our fliers? It's the reward money we'd offered. I have to say you've more than earned it." I'd barely gotten my "thank you" out when she turned to the audience and announced, "This young man saved my baby with the breath of life." She was gesturing to me like I was a washer-dryer combo on *The Price is Right*. "From what I've been told, he's a bona fide hero!"

Applause. More flashbulbs. I held up the check for the audience to see while my leg was still under heavy attack. I swear it was like we were putting on the strangest show on Earth. "Mon Dieu! Shatzi, nein. Nein!" Mrs. Futterman scolded, pulling the dog off me. He whimpered and whined as she led him offstage.

"Well, this is all real sentimental-like," that Otis guy complained, scooting through his row, "but it ain't solved diddly. I'm going home to watch the Bears game, but as far as I'm concerned this war ain't over – it's only begun."

"Wait!" I lunged for the podium. Divine inspiration was showering down on me and I had to act fast before I had time to reconsider. "Okay, here's the deal. Whoever took the spotlight, returns it with no questions asked. Got it?" I looked over at Zack to make sure he was listening. He was. "Promise you'll let us put on our production of *Oliver!* with no picketing, no – pot banging . . . and I – I sign this check over to the Fireballs right now. To buy a scoreboard, or uniforms, or whatever the heck you guys want!"

I couldn't believe what had just come out of my mouth – but it turned out to be a real crowd-pleaser. Even Shatzi was barking from the wings.

"A measly grand ain't gonna solve nothing," Mr. Kincaid snarled, jumping to his feet. Zack yanked him right back down with "Give him a freakin' break, Dad!"

"It's a start, Mr. Kincaid," I said with a steady gaze. "Look, if a Doberman pinscher and a poodle can coexist peacefully in the same dog, why can't sports and culture coexist peacefully in the same town?"

"Oh, brother!" Darlene spouted. "You really stink with those metaphors."

Okay, not exactly Shakespeare. But before the week was out, that idiotic quote would appear in the *Penny Pincher,* the *Buttermilk Falls Bugle,* and the *Hinkleyville Herald.* (Stick it, Darlene!) Right under a photo of me holding the check in my "Give Peas a Chance" sweatshirt, with Shatzi doing the dance-of-love on my leg.

Chapter 21

Something Borrowed, Something Blue

"Happy wedding day!"

"Oh, Dustin, you scared the bejesus out of me," Aunt Olive said, clutching the top of her robe. "But don't you look dapper in your blue tweed suit."

"Blue!" Aunt Birdie exclaimed. Her hair was piled a mile high and she was frantically picking threads off the wedding dress, which was spread out across the bed. "You've got Nana Grubbs's lace hanky for your something old, and your dress is new – but you need something blue, Olive."

"How about my varicose veins?" They both erupted in a glass-shattering cackle.

"We'll *all* be turning blue if it gets any colder outside," Aunt Birdie added.

I was already blue – both inside and out. Being back in the play and everything (whatever the role) gave my spirits a boost, but the Dad incident was still gnawing away at my guts. As my aunts were in a tailspin muttering "blue-blue-blue," it dawned on me that it was perfect timing to present my gift.

"I didn't have time to wrap it," I said, snatching the tiny, white box from my pocket and plucking off the lid, "but will this do?" My aunts turned to look.

"Oh!" Aunt Olive gushed. Her cheeks went wet with tears faster than her hand could cover her mouth. "It's breathtaking."

The blue crystals on the dragonfly pin did look awesome, glimmering against the purple, velvet lining. Aunt Olive pinned it onto the jacket of her dress, then pinned me in one of her bear hugs. They usually made me squirmy – but with her moving to Hinkleyville in a matter of hours, I didn't want this one to stop.

"Okay, Olive, pull yourself together." Aunt Birdie took her by the arm and sat her in front of the vanity mirror. "Let's get your wiglet attached right now so we have time to squeeze you into that girdle."

That was my cue to leave. "What about Granny?" I whispered on my way into the hall. "Is she still acting all – crotchety?"

"Does a woodpecker squat in the woods?" Aunt Birdie mumbled through the clump of hairpins poking out of her mouth. "Haven't seen hide nor seek of her all morning."

I was just going to walk right by Granny's bedroom door.

Having to fake a happy face all day was going to be hard enough without her giving me grief. But something made me grit my teeth and knock.

"Gran?" I said. "It's me, Dustin. You decent?"

I pushed the door open a crack and peeked inside. The usual rubbing alcohol smell of her room was camouflaged by heavy perfume. "Are you sleeping?" No answer. It was dark, but I could still see a crown of silver braids sticking out from the covers. *Something's definitely up.* I knew I was asking for it, but I took a deep breath and whipped off her blanket in a single throw.

"Hey!" Granny screeched, springing to life.

She was wearing her navy blue church dress and the good stockings that go all the way up. Plus, her false teeth were in her mouth ready for action.

"You've changed your mind," I said, grinning. "You're coming to the wedding!"

"Nobody said no such thing."

"Well, today's not Sunday, so why are you so dressed up?"

"In case I die in my sleep, I'll be all ready to ship to the funeral parlor."

"Don't kid a kidder, kid. You're busted."

"*Humph!*" she replied, and pulled the covers back over herself.

I stared down at her for the longest time, waiting for something to happen. But nothing did. Finally I'd had it.

"When's it gonna sink in?" I yelled, ripping open the drapes. A tornado of dust specks swirled through the air. "This is it! Aunt Olive's getting married today and moving away and there's not a doggone thing you can do to change that. Zilch, nada, nothin'. So you can either be Granny Grudge and lock yourself in your room all day, tearing yourself up inside – or join the party."

Her usual response would have been to go for the jugular. But she just lay there blinking up at the ceiling. "It's your choice," I jabbed, storming out of her room. "But either way, she's still leaving."

I slammed the door and stepped into what had transformed into Grand Central Station. On my way into the kitchen, a mishmash of flowers, food, and people whizzed past me: the butcher, the baker, the finger-food maker. Aunt Birdie was already at the open refrigerator, strapping on a wrist corsage and barking orders at the caterers. Foil-covered trays lined the counters, and there were smelly, mystery-meat UFOs smoking on the stove – Unidentified Frying Objects.

"Uh-oh! Aunt Birdie, have you seen the cat?"

"Oh, Ellen picked Cinnamon up early this morning. I tell ya, I'm sure gonna miss that li'l pussy-puss-puss."

"LMNOP is back?"

I snatched a deviled egg from a tray and popped it into my mouth just as Father Downing was squeezing by, carrying a Bible, earmuffs, and a steaming coffee-to-go cup.

"Am I headed in the right direction?" he asked.

"Yeah, out back," I told him, swallowing fast. "Hang a left at the compost heap and aim for the frozen guests. Break a leg, Father."

"Olive, the priest is here!" Aunt Birdie called out. "Chop-chop!"

"Say, I understand you really shook things up at the high school today," he said as he weaved through the wedding workers. "Quite a noble gesture, sacrificing that check the way you did."

"Thanks. Chock it up to temporary insanity." *It's a good thing it all happened so fast – that grand would've really come in handy.* I waited until he was out of earshot and the back door banged before turning to Aunt Birdie, who was still at the fridge messing with the bouquets. "Man, how did he catch word already? Is there, like, a hotline to St. Agatha's?"

"Oh, you know how things are in Buttermilk Falls," she muttered. "News spreads faster than wildflowers."

"Wild*fire*," I said, correcting her as usual.

"What?"

"Fire, Aunt Birdie," I yelled. *"Fire!"*

"Oh, my God!" she cried, tossing the bridal bouquet into the air. "Dustin, go grab your grandma! Nobody panic! Remember, stop, rock 'n' roll!"

"Stop, *drop,* and roll."

Luckily, I'd set things straight before she hit the floor.

* * *

It wasn't until I'd already escorted Aunt Olive halfway down the makeshift aisle in the backyard, heading for her shivering groom, when I realized where "The Wedding March" was coming from. Opus Five! Wally and the rest of his quintet were set up in front of the lawn-mower shed. *How could he not even bother telling me they were gigging in my own backyard? The ultimate slap in the face.* I was glaring at the Oxymoron, hoping his lips would get frozen stuck to his horn, when my aunt whispered, "Thanks so much for doing this, sweetheart."

"Not a problem." *Little did she know.* I guess it was worth it, though – she looked so happy. The blushing bride, gliding down the aisle. Well, not so much blushing as windburned – and not so much gliding either. Her heels kept sinking into the ground with every step. When we reached the rickety trellis, I handed her off to the bug man of her dreams, then parked myself on an ice-cold folding chair next to Mom.

"We are gathered here on this bone-shatteringly brisk autumn day," Father Downing began through trembling lips, "to join this man and this woman in holy matrimony . . ."

My focus shifted from his words to the bottom of Aunt Olive's dress. Apparently she'd dragged a bushel's worth of dead leaves along with her. *Funny. But sad.* It made me think about how her marriage was just getting started while Mom and Dad's was lying in a dried-up heap.

"I saw you and Dad getting kind of touchy-feely through

the window of the motel," I muttered into Mom's coat sleeve. "Holding hands and stuff. What was that about?"

"Hmm? Oh. Not now."

"C'mon, tell me."

She did up her fake-fur collar. "If you must know, we were just discussing Gordy's last-minute college plans – and how we were going to work things out financially. We certainly didn't see that one coming."

"Oh." Mom handed me a tissue and I emptied my drippy nose. "You must really hate him now, huh?"

"Hate who?"

"China's prime minister," I said sarcastically. "Dad!"

"Oh, honey, I'll always love your father." Her answer, like the wind, just about blew me away. "Just because he makes me want to strangle him from time to time doesn't mean I don't love him – I just can't live with him. He is who he is and he's never gonna change. Like they say, a leopard never loses its spots. Now shush."

She was right about the spots thing. Teddy Grubbs *was* who he was – love him or leave him. Or both in Mom's case. She took my gloved hand in hers and suddenly the sun broke through and everything shimmered in a silvery sheen. The weather and my father had something in common: They were both totally unpredictable.

As Father Downing was speed-preaching toward the big

finish, I heard the sound of crunching leaves coming from behind. It turned out to be Granny wrapped in a blanket, scurrying down the aisle. *Jeez, if the acting thing doesn't work out I should become a motivational speaker!* I laughed out loud when I noticed the Vegas-showgirl earrings she was sporting. Her earlobes were swinging low from the weight – they reminded me of the pounded-out chicken breasts Aunt Olive used for her chicken piccata.

"Do you, Olive Tallulah Grubbs, take Dennis Peter Smashum to be your lawfully wedded husband?"

Tallulah?

"I do," the bride-cicle said through a tiny cloud puff.

"What?" Father Downing asked.

Aunt Olive lifted one of his earmuffs and repeated, *"I do!"*

The knot had been officially tied and the guests rushed into the house to thaw out and chow down. Wally and his new best friend attempted to make small talk with me while they were stuffing their faces at the buffet table, but I wasn't buying it. "You should ask to make sure the hired help is allowed to eat," was my only comment. But I refused to let them bum me out. *People are who they are and there's not a darn thing you can do about it.* So after three plates of food, I undid my belt buckle and did what any red-blooded American boy would do. The Hokey Pokey. Just as we got to the "turn yourself around" part, the phone rang and I made a mad dash to answer it.

"That's what it's all about!" I sang into the receiver.

"Turn on channel five quick!" It was LMNOP.

"*Err* – I'm kinda in the middle of a wedding reception here."

"Omigod, quick, quick!"

With phone in hand, I flew over to the television set and clicked it on – luckily, it was already tuned to channel five.

"Yeah? So? There's some guy tripping over a Chihuahua," I told her. "What's the big deal?"

"Nuts," LMNOP said. "You just missed your television debut on *America's Goofiest Slips and Trips*!"

"Wait. Say that again."

"They showed a video of you singing in the shower and taking a nosedive. I'm serious! I think it was that same night I brought Cinnamon –"

"Cripes!" I slammed down the phone and turned to Gordy's deejay setup. "Hey, turdface," I yelled over a roomful of distant relatives who had their left hands in and were shaking them all about. "Please tell me you didn't send in that tape of me half-naked in the shower to that *America's Goofiest* show! Is that why you got that letter from NBC? Gooord!"

"Huh? Oh, right, I forgot," he said, switching off the boom box. "Was that on tonight? Surprise!" And switched it back on.

I needed some fresh air before I rearranged his face! So I grabbed a jacket off the coatrack and made a quick exit onto the front porch. *That wasn't exactly the television debut I was hoping for – far from it!* My life wasn't turning out at all like it was supposed to. And my patience, like the pages of this book, was quickly running out.

"Where's my happy ending?" I shouted up at the moon, struggling into the jacket. I collapsed onto the porch bench just as LMNOP was climbing the front steps.

"It was the freakiest thing, seeing you on TV like that. "Look," she said, showing me her hands, "I'm still trembling."

"That's 'cause it's colder than a witch's spit out here. I didn't win anything, did I?"

She shook her head no and plopped down on the bench next to me. Just then the front door squeaked open and Opus Five started filing past us, lugging their instrument cases. The Walrus was the last one out. He stopped right in front of me and I felt my buttocks clench.

"Uh, that's my jacket," he said, staring me in the face. "It's new."

The pound and a half of miniquiches stuffed in the pockets should've tipped me off. I quickly got out of the denim tarp and tossed it to him.

"I heard about that town meeting today," he muttered, galumping down the steps. "That you stuck up for all the artsy kids – musicians too. Pretty cool."

"Yeah, well – no biggie." I must've been a little dumbstruck by his verbal pat on the back. It wasn't until he was headed down Cubberly that it occurred to me to return the compliment with "You guys sounded great tonight!"

"Thanks," Wally shouted, practically stumbling over his own feet. "Hero."

"I'll call you later!"

We said it in unison. I wondered if either one of us would follow through on that anytime soon. Still, it felt good.

"What meeting?" LMNOP asked. She grabbed the mildew-scented quilt hanging over the seatback and flung it over the both of us. That felt good too. "Did I miss anything exciting while I was away?"

"Nah. Same old, same old."

"Liar. Well, you'll fill me in later. So . . . notice anything different about *me*? No more braces!" She blurted it out before I could guess. I had to admit, she did look semidecent for a change. More mature or something. And hardly any lisp. "Left 'em back in Gloucester. Along with my father."

"Oh, yeah." I remembered her last postcard. "Sorry."

"He'll be back. At least for Christmas."

That was debatable, but I kept it to myself. Dads were a touchy subject any way you looked at it. We sat silent and shivering for quite a while, staring at the three-quarter moon, until – *Ka-boom!* Both of us jumped and practically hit the porch roof when an explosion came from the backyard. A bright red blaze lit up the treetops.

"What the heck was that?" LMNOP said, hugging her knees.

"Fireworks."

"Oooh! I love pyrotechnics."

"Gordy's probably setting them off in the empty lot behind the garage. Mom's gonna annihilate him. It'll save me the trouble."

"Ah, you should cut your brother some slack." I was about to tell her to mind her own business, until she finished with, "It can't be easy having such an extraordinary little brother."

The fireworks were really going to town – making it impossible to talk. Weird how I actually wanted our conversation to continue even though I felt like a human ice sculpture. "She's good people," like Granny would say. *Who knew?* For the first time ever I was happy to be her friend. All of a sudden LMNOP threw off the quilt, grabbed my hand and pulled me down the steps to get a better view of the sky, which was exploding in green, red, and white sunbursts.

"C'mon!" she urged, running toward the backyard, where the guests were spilling onto the lawn.

Out of the corner of my eye I saw a streak of blue light that stopped me in my tracks. Not in the sky, though. This was whizzing down the street. When I turned around, I swore I was hallucinating. A taxi with a blue LuvQUEST.com sign glowing on the roof was pulling up behind the carnation-covered station wagon in our driveway. My heart thundered louder than the fireworks.

Ka-boom!

I stood watching and waiting for the engine to turn off, but it kept on running and running. Finally it stopped and the cab door swung open.

"A funny thing happened on the way to Orlando," I heard. *Whoosh! Ka-boom!*

It was one of those rare perfect moments. I wanted to remember that feeling forever. Bottle it. Freeze it, like Aunt Olive did with the top layer of wedding cake. Don't get me wrong. There weren't any major expectations going on inside my head, watching Dad get out of his cab – I mean, I'm not stupid. But I did have a million questions.

"I switched flights," he said. "SeaWorld gave me a little leeway. As long as I can get there on Monday the job is still mine."

And with that, he'd answered about half of them – and raised a half dozen more. Dad stood staring up at the house and squeezing my shoulder. "Wow 'em with a big finish and they'll forgive ya for anything. Right, kid?"

"Right, kid."

I guess he was about to put that to the test. He was mumbling something about finally facing the music when the cell phone in his other hand started squawking. "Oh. Here," he said, handing it to me. "Someone wants to talk to you."

"Huh? Who?" I put the phone to my ear, watching Dad trudge toward the front porch. "Hello?"

"Dustin? Hi! I thought we lost our connection. It's Nadine

Fleck, your father's agent. I wanted to speak to you personally to give you the news."

"News?" I asked through chattering teeth.

"Tell me, are you a big fan of our national pastime?"

"Sure. Who doesn't like watching TV?"

"Oh, you are such a hoot," she said, chuckling. "No, I mean baseball! McKenna Casting thinks you'd be perfect for a new commercial they're working on. It's for Toyco's Pop-Up Pitcher . . ."

While she was feeding me the details I fell cross-legged onto the cold grass, laughing to myself. I looked up past the branches, through the purplish smoke at the milky-white moon that was hogging the sky. Even though a chunk was missing, it was plump and complete. "Thank you," I mouthed.

And right on cue something wet landed in my eye.

"Bah-*dum*-pum!" I said with a wink.

Acknowledgments

Will the following people please rise and take a well-deserved bow for their selfless contributions to this book: Andrea Spooner, Sangeeta Mehta, Steven Chudney, Chris Woodworth, Lisa Williams Kline, Jeffrey Kline, DVM, Tracy Shaw, Alexandra Speck, and Mary-Ann Trippet. (Okay, you can sit down now – people are staring.)

Don't Miss

Dustin Grubbs
ONE★MAN SHOW

Now available in paperback

John J. Bonk, the author of *Dustin Grubbs: One-Man Show*, previously worked as a singer, tap dancer, and actor in New York and around the world. He has now hung up his tap shoes, focusing his creative energy on "performing on the page." John J. Bonk lives in New York City.